I0680935

THE FAIRY CROSSES OF
FANNIN COUNTY

THE FAIRY CROSSES OF FANNIN COUNTY

JACLYN WELDON WHITE

Deeds Publishing | Atlanta

Published by Deeds Publishing in Athens, GA
www.deedspublishing.com

Printed in The United States of America

Cover design and text layout by Mark Babcock

Library of Congress Cataloging-in-Publications data is available upon request.

ISBN 978-1-947309-65-4

Books are available in quantity for promotional or premium use. For information, email info@deedspublishing.com.

First Edition, 2019

10 9 8 7 6 5 4 3 2 1

To Dale Cramer, Jackie K. Cooper, and Milam Propst,
dear friends and fellow word warriors.

ONE

THE SOUND OF SOMEONE MOVING QUIETLY IN THE DIM ROOM
was what woke me. I opened my eyes and was rewarded with a view
of Nick Buckley's nicely-muscled bare back.

"Good morning."

He turned and gave me a smile. "Good morning to you, too.
Sorry, didn't mean to wake you. I was trying to be quiet."

I yawned. "What time is it? Is the sun even up?"

He glanced at the window where faint light showed around the
closed blinds. "Will be in a few minutes. It's just past seven."

It seemed earlier. Actually, it *was* earlier. We'd only moved from
standard to daylight savings time three weeks before. And while I
loved having the daylight last longer in the evenings, I was no fan of
the later sunrises. But it would all even out in a couple of months
with summer's arrival.

Nick sat on the side of the bed and ran two fingers from my
shoulder to my hand, producing a nice little shiver of pleasure. I
scooted closer to him.

"The bed's nice and warm." I patted his pillow and smiled invit-
ingly. "Don't you have just a little time to spare?"

He laughed. "I wish I did." He leaned over and gave me a sweet kiss, then got to his feet. "But I've got a plane to catch."

"I know," I said with a sigh. "Just how long is a flight from Atlanta to Vancouver?"

He pulled on a shirt and began buttoning it. "About 7 hours —counting the layover in Salt Lake. I'll call you when I get there."

He owned a commercial real estate development company. Although he told people he was semi-retired and that his son, Jonathan now ran the business, Nick hadn't been able to completely let go. He still got involved in projects that interested him and the multi-use development they were planning and building in Vancouver was one of those projects.

Another quick kiss and he was gone. A moment later, the front door opened, closed, and I heard the key turn in the lock. Nick had already packed a bag that was waiting for him in his house—just across the cul-de-sac from mine.

Nick and I had met when he moved into the neighborhood the previous November. The spark was immediate and we'd been together for several months now. I'd never been happier and expected to spend the rest of my life with this remarkable man. I was sure he felt the same, but it was still a bit early for us to think about moving in together. So we continued to maintain our own houses.

Curtis, my brown tabby cat, jumped up and settled in what was his usual spot on the comforter at the foot of the bed. When Nick stayed over, Curtis was closed out of the bedroom. At first he'd complained loudly about the arrangement, yowling off and on at the door all night. But we'd determinedly ignored his behavior and now he accepted the banishment as an occasional inconvenience. But as soon as Nick left, he rushed into the bedroom to reclaim his rightful place.

I stretched and lay in the tangle of sheets for a few more minutes, watching the day brighten behind the blinds. The clock on the nightstand showed 7:40, early for a Sunday morning, but sleep was gone. By 8:15, I'd dressed, fed Curtis, had coffee going, and was considering my choices for breakfast. Curtis followed my every step in the kitchen — from the pantry, to the fridge and the table.

"I'm going to trip over you one of these days and we'll both get hurt," I told him as I nudged him out of the way with my foot.

I'd inherited the big cat when a neighbor passed away eight months before. It took some adjustment on both our parts, but we'd achieved an amiable living arrangement.

When I was seated at the kitchen table with a bagel and coffee, Curtis watched me for a minute, but soon gave up on the chance of my giving him any more to eat. He hopped up to the window sill where he could watch for chipmunks. and I thought about what to do with the rest of my day. The house was clean, Nick was on his way to the airport, and I'd finished my week's work. Then the phone rang.

"You've got to help me, Emily!"

For a split second I didn't recognize the voice, then realized it was Owen — Owen Christopher, my ex-husband.

"What are you talking about?"

"I need help!" He did sound uncharacteristically upset. "Sarah's dead! Can you come to the house right now? The police are here and I'm pretty sure they think I did it! Emily, I need your help!"

I took a deep breath. "Why would you need *me*? You're the lawyer."

"Yeah, but you're the investigator. And you can find out what's going on. The cops know you — they like you. They'll sure as hell talk to you more than they will to me."

I was tempted to hang up. While the news of Sarah's death was shocking, it didn't exactly stagger me with grief. We'd been good friends years ago, but that was before I found her with my husband in our bed. And, with that history, I sure didn't owe Owen anything.

"Emily, *please!*" It was the closest I'd ever heard him come to begging. And he *was* the father of my children. Chelsea and Drew would certainly want me to help him.

"Okay," I said after a moment's pause. "I'll come."

"*Hurry!*"

TWO

I DIDN'T WASTE TIME, BUT I DIDN'T EXACTLY HURRY. I KNEW from long experience that it takes hours for the police to work a crime scene. I'd worked my share of them during my tenure with the Blount County Police Department.

After I brushed my hair—brown, chin length, with a generous sprinkling of gray—I took the time to put on a little make up, then frowned at the image in the mirror. At 58, I didn't expect to look 40, but in my weaker moments I wished I did.

Curtis followed me to the back door, matching me step by step, yowling pitifully. He didn't like it when I left the house and his objections were getting worse. I wondered if he'd developed some kind of feline separation anxiety.

"Sorry, big guy. Gotta go."

There was a lot of activity in the neighborhood that early April morning. The nice weather had lured numerous joggers and walkers outside. I waved to Tricia Thompson, who was strolling along with her golden retriever, Barney. On the next block, Mark and Leslie Geoghegan were walking hand in hand and, across from them, Leo Montgomery was energetically racking up steps. I lifted a hand to greet the Andersons, but I didn't bother waving at Leo. He was a dedicated walker and would say hello if you spoke first, but he never seemed interested in interacting with his neighbors. He hardly ever looked up from the pavement in front of him.

Driving slowly along the tree-lined streets, I let the windows down and breathed in the cool spring air. Everywhere I looked, something was blooming. Snapdragons and lilies competed for attention with daffodils, tulips, and early roses. The yoshino cherry trees were a riot of pink and white.

Marchpoint Manse is an over-55, active adult community northeast of Atlanta, in the rolling foothills of the Appalachian Mountains. It's a good-sized place with nearly 900 houses, divided into three sections determined by the size and cost of the houses. The smallest—two bedrooms, two baths and an office—are in The Village, where I lived. Houses in The Meadows have three bedrooms and larger living spaces. The Arbor, which takes up most of the area on the ridge at the back of the neighborhood, contains the largest and most expensive homes, with four bedrooms, formal dining rooms, and some finished basements.

The designs of the houses here weren't unique. Similar lots and floor plans could be found in most every subdivision in the Atlanta area. But people didn't come here for the homes. They came for the amenities. Marchpoint boasts a huge clubhouse, a gym, several pools, tennis courts, and hiking trails, and backs up to a golf course. It's pretty close to living in a resort.

After Owen and I divorced, I lived in an apartment for a couple of years. Then last June, I'd moved here. It seemed like the perfect place for me—a small house with little upkeep, an HOA that provided yard maintenance, friendly people, and as many activities as

I wanted to take advantage of. I loved the neighborhood and the people.

Then, five months ago, Owen and Sarah had relocated here. The house they bought was, of course, one of the most expensive ones in The Arbor. Moving here was a tacky thing for them to do and I was certain the move had been Sarah's idea. After Owen and I split up, a number of our friends had dropped her. I suspected this was her way of showing me she was the ultimate winner.

It really bothered me for a while. But Marchpoint was a large community and our paths rarely crossed. Since Nick and I had been together, I'd hardly given them a passing thought.

The drive to Blackberry Ridge took about five minutes. I was especially careful at the stop signs since a number of our residents consider traffic laws suggestions rather than rules. Each month there were several wrecks at these intersections.

Even if I hadn't already known, it wouldn't have been hard to figure out which house was Owen's. It looked like the circus was in town. Three uniformed officers stood talking in the front yard. Clusters of neighbors gathered in adjoining yards and on the sidewalks up and down the street. I was sure more were following the activities from behind their curtains. Two patrol cars sat in Owen's driveway and a crime scene truck, an unmarked dark blue sedan, and the medical examiner's van were all parked on the street in front of the house. I pulled up behind the van and got out.

Across the street, Anna Lumpkin stood on her front porch, watching the comings and goings at Owen's house. I didn't know her well, but we'd taken a couple of yoga classes together. I waved and she waved back.

"Emily Christopher! It's kind of early for the DA's Office to get interested in a case."

I turned to see a tall, very thin man in uniform. It was Mike Carlton, who I'd known for over 20 years. We'd first met when he was a patrolman, fresh out of the academy. Now he was a uniform captain, probably only a few years away from retirement.

"Hey, Mike. No, I'm not here officially. I live here."

His brows drew up in a confused frown. "Here?"

"No, not *here*. I live in the neighborhood." I gestured toward the house with my head. "But my ex-husband lives here. He called and asked me to come."

He looked uncomfortable. "You know that his—umm—his wife is dead?"

"Yeah. He called me. Seems to think I can help." I glanced at the blue sedan. "Who caught the case?"

"Engels and Webster."

That was good and bad news. Buddy Webster and I had been friends for years, starting our careers together in patrol and working side by side in the Detective Division. Beth Engels, on the other hand, was about 10 years younger than Buddy and had never had any use for me. I have to admit that the feeling was mutual.

"Do you think that I could see Owen for a few minutes?"

Mike turned his body away from me and spoke into the radio on his shoulder, so quietly I couldn't hear what he said. A moment later he got a reply.

He turned back. "I think he's giving a statement right now, but Webster says to come to the front door and he'll talk to you."

I followed the drive and walkway to a small front porch. Two white wicker rocking chairs and a small table were grouped to one side, giving it a homey look. As I climbed the two steps, I noticed the ceiling had been painted a pale blue and wondered if the HOA knew about that. It surely must have violated some neighborhood regulation.

The door opened before I could knock and Buddy Webster stepped out, smiling. He left the door open behind him, but all that was visible was the foyer.

"Emily, you're looking great!" A smile lit his florid face. "How have you been?"

"Doing good, Buddy. How about you?"

He shrugged his big shoulders. "Can't complain." Then, with the pleasantries over, he went straight to it. "I didn't expect to see you here."

"Owen called and asked me to come. He sounded bad."

"He should sound bad. His wife is dead and he was the only one here. No sign of anyone else in the house and no forced entry. And he says he didn't hear anything. Just found her when he got up this morning." The last part was delivered with exaggerated disbelief.

I digested that information, then asked, "What happened? Did she fall or something? Was it an accident?"

He shook his head. "Not likely. This one's definitely a homicide."

"I can't believe Owen could hurt anyone ..."

"Come on, Emily. You've never been sentimental." He looked over my shoulder to where a man and woman in official-looking coveralls were pulling a gurney out of the back of the medical examiner's van. "You know anyone can do damn near anything under the right circumstances. How many people have we arrested that everyone said couldn't hurt anyone?"

I didn't have a good answer for that. I knew he was right.

He looked back at me. "And I don't understand why he called *you*. I mean, when y'all broke up, he was the one who caused it, wasn't he? I'd think you'd be the last person he'd think would help him."

"I think he just wanted someone he knew to be here. Besides, I live in the neighborhood."

"Well, from what I saw, it's a mess. Not sure how you can help him with this."

I wasn't either, but I was here so I might as well see what I could do. "Can I see him? Just for a couple of minutes?"

He leaned back against the door frame. "Not right now. Engels is questioning him. It could be a while."

If they really thought he'd killed her, it might be a long time before I could see him.

Webster's eyes narrowed in speculation. "How well did you know the victim, Emily?"

The tone was familiar and I should have expected it. He was considering me as a suspect. And why not? I certainly had motive. She'd destroyed my marriage.

"I used to know Sarah real well, before she and Owen got together. But not at all lately."

"It's hard to believe they moved into your neighborhood," he said thoughtfully. "You were here first, weren't you?"

I laughed. "I was. And I thought it was a nasty thing for them to do."

"I can imagine. You must have been furious."

"Oh, yeah. Maybe worse than that. But I got over it. And I sure didn't have anything to do with her death."

He looked uncomfortable. "I hate this, but I still need to know —"

"Of course, you have to ask, Buddy. I'll make it as easy on you as I can. What time period are we talking about?"

"Let's go with the last twelve hours."

"That's simple, then. I was with my... my friend, Nick Buckley."

"All night?"

I couldn't help smiling. "Yes, all day yesterday and all night. We spent yesterday at a festival in Roswell, then had dinner in Marinville with friends. We got home to my house about nine. And Nick stayed at my house last night, left about seven this morning. He's flying to Vancouver today, but you can probably catch him before he boards the flight."

I recited Nick's phone number, which Webster duly wrote in a small notebook. "And if you need it, I can find the contact info on the friends we were with last night."

"We can hold off on that for now."

I looked past him into the house. "Any chance I could see the crime scene?"

He hesitated a minute, then shrugged. "Yeah, I guess so. Come on in."

The foyer was spacious, furnished with a walnut console table that held a pottery platter, a stack of mail, and two candles. Beyond the entry way was a dining room, kitchen, and living room. The house was beautifully and expensively furnished — exactly what I'd expect from Sarah. The only thing out of place was the body in the office to our right.

Sarah was sprawled on the floor near the built-in bookcases

on the far wall. She wore a short red dress and high-heeled black pumps, or at least one high-heeled pump. The second one lay several inches from her bare left foot. A pool of blood surrounded her upper body. Even at that distance, I could see the horrible damage to her head.

"There she is," Webster said unnecessarily.

To the right of her body were several small gray stones and an overturned wooden bowl. On the left were two sizable pieces of what looked like pink rock which I recognized as one of those salt block lamps, now broken. There were dark stains on one piece.

"Murder weapon?" I asked.

"Yeah, looks like it. I'd say somebody used it to smash her head in."

"Think it would have taken a lot of strength?"

He shook his head. "Well, if you were strong enough to lift it up in the first place, the rest would be easy."

"And no sign of forced entry?"

He shook his head. "No. Except for this room, nothing seems out of place in the whole house."

In the office, crime scene techs busily went about their work, printing various surfaces and photographing everything in sight while the man and woman from the Medical Examiner's Office waited at one side.

At a signal from one of the techs, the ME people came forward. They carefully lifted Sarah onto the gurney and zipped the body bag closed around her. A moment later, they wheeled her out. It was a sad ending and I almost felt sorry for her.

THREE

THE SOUND OF VOICES, QUIET AND CONVERSATIONAL, CAME
from the direction of a hallway off the right side of the living
room. A moment later Beth Engels appeared with Owen following in her wake. Owen has always looked just the way an attorney
should—tall, trim, serious, with glasses. The passing of time had
only intensified that impression. He appeared more distinguished
at 60 than he had in his 30s and 40s.

This morning, however, he resembled a loser in a barroom brawl
more than a respected member of the bar. In jeans and a rumpled
polo shirt that looked like he'd grabbed out of the dirty clothes
hamper, his hair was uncombed and his jaw covered with a gray
stubble.

He trailed behind Engels like a scolded puppy, but when he
looked up and saw me, there was a flash of hope in his eyes.

"Emily!" He hurried over to where I stood. He looked like he
was moving in for a hug, but my expression and the backward step
I took put an end to that idea. "Thank God, you're here!"

Beth Engels—tall, brunette, with the big-shouldered body of a
swimmer—didn't share his joy. She glared at me, then deliberately
turned and walked into the office where two technicians were still

at work. Buddy joined her there, leaving me alone with my ex-husband.

I wasn't surprised that she didn't acknowledge me. A few years before, when I'd been working as an investigator for the District Attorney's Office, one of her cases—a felony theft—landed on my desk. Her work had been sloppy and I'd found numerous mistakes and omissions. Because of that, the DA declined to prosecute. Since then she'd been actively hostile toward me, as if I were to blame for her shoddy work.

Owen glanced into the office and seemed relieved that Sarah's body had been removed. "They think *I* did it," he told me in a low voice. "How can they think *I* did it?"

"Spouses are always the first suspects," I told him. "You know that. At least they haven't charged you."

"Yeah, not yet. But I have to go to police headquarters to make a formal statement."

"You know that's routine, too." I looked over at Engels, deep in conversation with Webster. Maybe we had time for a couple of questions. "Can you tell me what happened?"

"When I got up this morning I found her, just lying in there, blood everywhere. And that stupid pink lamp next to her. I've hated it since she bought it, but it was supposed to purify the air or something." He turned his head and swallowed hard. "I ... you could tell she was ... dead. Her eyes just open and ... well ... just dead. I don't know what happened. I never heard anything. And it doesn't look like anything's missing."

"Has Sarah been any different lately? Strange or upset about anything?"

"Yeah." He glanced at the two detectives. Engels pointed at us

14

and, even though she was speaking too low for me to hear, it was obvious she was not happy about my presence at her crime scene.

"There's too much to go into right now," Owen said hurriedly. "Can we talk later, when I get back?"

I reflected that he might not be coming back if they arrested him, but I didn't say it out loud. "Did Sarah say anything when you went to bed last night? I mean, it's strange. She looks like she's dressed for a party."

He pushed out a breath. "She…ummm…she wasn't here when I went to bed."

What did that mean? I started to ask, but the detectives were moving our way.

"It's time to go," Engels told Owen.

He moved with her towards the door. Webster and I followed behind.

Once outside, the three of them walked to the unmarked sedan. Owen climbed awkwardly into the backseat, pulling the door closed behind him. A minute later, they drove away, weaving through the official vehicles and the crowd of curious neighbors that seemed to have doubled in the time I'd been inside the house.

I waved to Mike Carlton and, after managing to turn around on the crowded block, left the area myself. My phone started ringing as I pulled into the garage. It was Nick.

"Why are the police checking up on you?" He sounded concerned, but also distracted. I could hear public address voices in the background.

I explained as quickly as I could.

"They don't seriously believe *you* had anything to do with that woman's death?"

"No, I don't think so. Especially if you provided me with an alibi."

He gave a little laugh. "I did, since I was in a unique position to do so."

I smiled. "You certainly were. As I recall, you were in several unique positions."

He chuckled. "You shouldn't talk like that to a man standing in the middle of a busy airport." Then he became serious again. "But I don't understand why you're even involved. I mean, you and Owen sure aren't on the best of terms —"

"No, but we were married for a lot of years and then there are the kids. If I can help, I feel like I have to."

He sighed. "Of course, you do. I understand, at least I think so." I heard a woman's voice in the background. "Gotta go. They just called my flight. I'll talk to you tonight."

"Travel safe."

FOUR

CURTIS GREETED ME AT THE BACK DOOR WITH A FEW INDIG-
nant meows. He seemed to hate it more every time I left the house.
I wondered if leaving music or the TV on would make him feel
less alone. I gave him a good head scratching and it mollified him
enough that he could leave my side and wander over to his dry food
bowl.

It was only mid-morning, but it seemed much later. I'd foolishly
told Owen that we'd talk when he got home which effectively put
me on call, waiting for him. Even if the police only questioned him
and took a written statement, it could be hours before they were
done. So I fixed a cup of coffee and turned on some music. A second
later, the sound of deep-voiced country filled the room. Sometimes,
you just need a little Garth.

In the office, I sat down at the computer. After checking my
email, I went over the reports I'd be turning in the next day. Two
burglaries and a few auto thefts, none of them were complicated. I
slipped the pages into a manila envelope and set them aside.

I couldn't stop thinking about Sarah and Owen. My emotions
were a crazy tangle. I guess if I'd ever really hated anyone, it was
Sarah Candler, now Christopher. For years we'd been close friends,

sharing confidences, talking nearly every day. We once even took a girls' vacation to Panama City and had a great time. I'd considered her one of my best friends until I discovered that she was having an affair with my husband. Of course, Owen had to share the blame. And it wasn't the first time he'd strayed. But it was Sarah's betrayal that had angered me the most.

But time had passed and I'd moved on. While I still had no use for her or him, those feelings of betrayal and loss had gradually faded. Of course, finding Nick Buckley probably had a lot to do with that, too. Just the thought of him now, on his way across the country, made me smile.

The doorbell rang as I was shutting down the computer. Curtis accompanied me to the front door, walking just inches ahead of me so that I had to be careful not to step on him. As we passed it, he took a sudden left into the kitchen, nearly bringing me down.

"If you trip me and kill me," I called after him as I kept walking, "there won't be anyone here to feed you and you'll die, too."

Linda Winkler stood on the porch. In a gauzy, bright yellow skirt and floral blouse, her long gray-blonde hair falling over her shoulders, she looked like the spirit of spring. Linda and I had been best friends in high school and, even though our personalities were nearly polar opposites, we'd remained close all the years since.

In fact, she was the reason I'd moved into Marchpoint. Six months after the death of her husband, she'd purchased one of the first houses built in the neighborhood. Her glowing descriptions of the place led me to give it a look several years later. I'd fallen in love with a house only half a block away from hers.

"Is it true?" she asked as soon as she stepped through the door.

It wasn't necessary to ask what she was talking about. Word

spreads fast in Marchpoint. "Well, it's true that Sarah Christopher was killed."

"And Owen was arrested?"

"No, he wasn't. He's just being questioned." I stepped into the kitchen. "Want some coffee?"

When she nodded, I filled the machine with water and popped in a coffee pod.

"What do you mean he hasn't been arrested? I heard they took him away in handcuffs!"

Yes, word spreads fast in Marchpoint, but it's not always accurate.

I told Linda what I knew. By the time I finished explaining what had happened, and that the police had taken Owen to headquarters so that he could make a formal statement, we were both settled in the living room, each sipping a fresh cup of coffee.

Through the sliding glass doors, I saw several bright yellow goldfinches vying for spots on the backyard feeder. Curtis, perched on the back of an easy chair, was watching them, too.

"Everybody's saying Owen killed her."

Of course, they were. And, although it wasn't an unreasonable assumption, it was premature.

"Nobody knows what happened yet. The police are still working the scene. They haven't charged anyone."

"Ummmmm. Not *yet*." She drank coffee. "And why did Owen call you? After what he did to you, how could he think you'd help him?"

I shrugged. "He sounded absolutely desperate and I didn't mind going over and seeing what I could find out. I knew some of the officers on the scene and they told me what they could. But it's so early in the investigation that my being there didn't really accomplish anything."

"Well, I hope they figure it out soon." She leaned forward and moved a couple of magazines from the coffee table to the floor. "Maybe we can learn something that will help." Then she reached in her bag and pulled out a deck of tarot cards, wrapped in a silk cloth. She shuffled the cards and began laying them out in a cross-like pattern. "This ought to tell us something."

I suppressed an impatient sigh. There was nothing I wanted to do less than watch Linda read her tarot cards, but I knew it was her way of dealing with problems. For as long as I'd known her, she'd been fascinated by all things paranormal. I, on the other hand, was a born skeptic. Somehow, in spite of our differences, we'd managed to remain close friends.

Linda has never met a psychic practice or idea she didn't embrace and, in the last few years, she'd turned that passion into a paying business. She owned a shop where she sold herbs, essential oils, fortune-telling paraphernalia, and tons of books dealing with the occult.

"I'm sure it will." It was easier to just agree when Linda got all mystical.

For half an hour, she studied the spread she'd laid out and interpreted the individual cards for me. I mostly listened to the music — satellite radio is a wonderful thing — and made brief, encouraging comments.

"Oh, yes, of course," Linda was saying. "The Queen of Swords reversed. An angry, manipulative woman; one who doesn't care about the rights of others." She looked at me. "Now who does that sound like?"

I shook my head. "Who?"

"Sarah, of course."

"Oh."

"And this is interesting, too."

Chris Stapleton was singing about a simple life. His wife Morgane's vocal harmony was so pure it almost brought tears to my eyes. It reminded me —

"Emily!"

"What?"

"I asked if you thought Sarah and Owen were happy."

I shrugged. "How would I know? I haven't talked to either of them in ages."

"Well, the Moon is prominent in this spread and that can indicate dishonesty, deceit, lies, insincerity."

I shook my head sadly. "They're both liars. I found that out the hard way."

My watch showed it was almost noon. It took Linda another ten minutes to wrap things up.

"Well, it looks to me like there was trouble in their marriage and one or both of them made some bad choices. Either anger or jealousy is probably to blame for Sarah's murder."

There was no point telling her that over half the murders committed every year were the result of anger or jealousy. Add greed and you had the homicidal trifecta.

"I'll keep that in mind," I said.

She nodded and started gathering up the cards. "I hope it helps. At least it got my mind off the HOA for a few minutes."

"Now what?" Marchpoint has a particularly aggressive Homeowners Association and every month seems to bring a new regulation.

"Roofs. Dirty roofs." She put the cards away and leaned back against the sofa.

"Huh?"

"That's right. We have to have our roofs pressure washed, because they're 'stained and unsightly.' And that's a direct quote. They've sent out a bunch of letters. I got mine yesterday." She drank more coffee which I thought must be cold by now. "I checked yours when I walked over and I'll bet you get a letter, too. The north side of your roof is pretty nasty."

"Who notices dirty roofs? I don't think I've ever even looked at them."

"Me, either, but evidently the HOA has looked a lot." She sighed. "So now I have to find somebody to clean it."

"Well, when you find somebody, give me the name. Sounds like I'm going to need some help, too."

Curtis abandoned his birdwatching, turned and made a graceful leap from the chair to the sofa, landing beside Linda. He snuggled up to her and she obligingly stroked his fur. His eyes closed in ecstasy and I could hear the purring from several feet away.

"You'd think they could find better things to do with their time," she said. "We've got a lot more serious problems in this neighborhood than dirty roofs."

"What serious problems?"

"Well, Sarah's murder, for one thing. If it isn't Owen, then any of us could be next!"

"I expect the police are going to wrap this up pretty quick."

Her eyes gleamed the way they do when she's about to deliver a particularly juicy bit of gossip. "And then there are the sex parties."

I'm not often speechless, but it took me more than a couple

of seconds to find the words. "Sex parties? What are you talking about?"

She leaned forward, hair falling around her face, to be sure I got every word. "I'm surprised you haven't heard. Everyone is talking about it. Once or twice a week, there's a secret party here in Marchpoint. Sometimes couples go, sometimes it's single people. Music, low lights — they go on until the wee hours of the morning!" She dropped her voice as if we she might be overheard. "They say sometimes young men are brought in. *Handsome* young men!"

"Where are these parties held?"

"Well, I don't know that for sure. Different houses on different nights, they say. I haven't talked to anyone who has actually *seen* one of the parties going on, but everybody's heard about them."

"I don't think that's anything to get too upset about. They're probably playing dominos or something."

Dominos are very big in Marchpoint.

We might have continued debating the existence of neighborhood orgies for some time, but Owen called.

"Can you come pick me up?"

I sighed. Of course, he was without a car because Engels and Webster had driven him to headquarters. They'd have also arranged to have him taken home, but, knowing Owen, I was sure he refused. One ride in a police car would have been enough. I could have said no, told him to call a friend or a ride service, but I didn't. I was already involved in the situation and we did have to talk about it.

"Yeah, I'll be there in about half an hour — outside the main entrance."

I explained to Linda that I had to leave.

"Yeah, I've got things to do, too," she said, getting to her feet. "By the way, Emily, did you send me a card?"

"A card? No. Why would I do that? It's not your birthday."

She reached in her big woven bag and pulled out a greeting card which she handed to me. On the front was a picture of a bouquet of flowers.

"Open it."

The inside was blank except for a brief handwritten message:

I am happy just knowing I am sharing
this beautiful world with you.

"That's sweet."

"I guess so," she said, "but it would be sweeter if it was signed."

"Maybe one of the kids sent it?"

She laughed. "Can you honestly see one of my guys writing that note to me?" Linda was mother to two sons, neither of which had ever been overly sentimental. "Besides, they'd have signed it if they sent it."

I gave it back to her. "Well, I'm sure you'll find out soon."

She paused at the door. "When I get home, I'm going to do another spread. And maybe cast some runes. We need to find out what's going on in this neighborhood."

Linda left to seek answers from the cosmos and I drove to police headquarters.

FIVE

OWEN LOOKED ABOUT HOW YOU'D EXPECT HIM TO AFTER finding his wife dead and being interrogated for several hours by the police. When he got into the car, I noticed his eyes were red-rimmed and his mouth was set in a hard line.

I actually felt a little sorry for him—but only a little. Not enough to erase all the hard feelings he'd created when he broke our family apart.

"Thank God, you're here, Emily."

I pulled away from the curb. "Buckle up. I can't drive with that warning bell going."

He obligingly reached for the seat belt. "You can't imagine what it's like in there! I was in this tiny room with no windows."

He'd obviously forgotten I'd spent fifteen years as a police detective, a lot of that time questioning people in just such a room.

"And, Em, they honestly think I killed her! How can they believe something so ridiculous? I couldn't kill anyone. I'm a *member of the bar*!"

Ah, there was that arrogance I was accustomed to. He was beginning to recover from his ordeal.

I bypassed the entrance to the expressway, preferring to take side roads. Nobody in the Atlanta area willingly takes the interstate if there's an alternative.

He rubbed a hand across his face. "I can't wait to get home and get a shower."

"Ummm...about that. I doubt if the police are through with your house yet."

"When will they be finished?" He sounded more than a little annoyed.

"They could be there for hours, maybe even a couple of days, before they release the scene."

"So what am I supposed to do?" he asked. "How can they do that? After all this and now I can't even go home?"

"Well, you could stay with a friend — "

He turned to look at me, an appealing expression on his face.

"Not a chance," I told him. "Maybe you could go to a hotel."

He blew out a breath, his irritation growing. "I don't even have my wallet with me. They dragged me out of my house with nothing."

"We can stop by your place. If you ask nicely, they'll probably let you pack a bag. They might even let you take your car."

We rode in silence for a while, then I asked, "So have you thought about the funeral?"

He looked stricken. "I...no...I haven't."

"Well, you need to. They'll be releasing her body in the next week or so."

"Oh, my God, I don't even know where to start."

I wasn't surprised. People—parents, assistants, business managers, wives, especially wives—had taken care of things for Owen all his life.

"Do what most people do, Owen. Choose a funeral home and call them. They'll walk you through it. You need to call Sarah's daughter, too. She's got to know what happened."

He sighed, overcome with his obligations.

"And she might help you with the funeral arrangements."

The possibility that someone else might deal with the unpleasantness he faced perked him up a little. "Yeah. I'll call her as soon as I can."

A young patrolman was sitting in his car in Owen's driveway. He got out when we approached the house and joined us on the front walk.

"Everyone's gone," he told us, "but they haven't released the scene yet."

Owen explained what he needed and the officer agreed to let him in the house, but with some restrictions.

"I have to go with you and you can't go into the office."

I waited outside. The block was still alive with people. Some had dogs with them, but most just stood around talking, their eyes frequently traveling to Owen's house. I noticed Anna Lumpkin was no longer alone. She'd been joined by two other women. The three were sitting on the porch, holding what looked to be glasses of iced tea. The scene of Sarah Christopher's murder had officially become neighborhood entertainment.

Owen emerged from the house after only a few minutes, a bag in his hand. But his car was another matter.

"I can't let you take it," the officer said, "not without an okay from the detectives."

Owen wasn't happy about that, but there wasn't any recourse. Back in the car, I offered to drive him to a hotel.

"Okay, but we need to talk first. I have to tell you what's been going on with Sarah. I want you to know everything." I really didn't want to know "everything" about Sarah and what was happening in their marriage, but I agreed to hear him out. We ended up in a coffee shop a few miles away. At 3:00 in the afternoon, it wasn't crowded. We ordered, got our coffee, and took a corner table well away from any other customers.

"Okay," I said after taking a sip of the drink I didn't want, "tell me."

"Things haven't been good for a couple of years. Guess we just kind of grew apart." He was having a hard time meeting my eyes. I knew it must have been awkward for him, admitting that life hadn't been perfect with the woman he'd left me for, but I wasn't interested in making it any easier.

"I thought it would be better after we moved into Marchpoint. Sarah was so excited about getting the house there. And it was good, at least for a while. She made some friends and got involved in the activities—yoga, water aerobics, she even started playing bridge, something she hadn't done since college. I thought she was happy, but a few months ago she started to change."

Two teenagers—coffee in one hand, phone in the other—took a table near us.

"Change how?"

He shook his head as if he wasn't sure how to explain. "She was growing more and more distant. She started spending a lot of time with her new friends—one in particular. Becky, Becky something. Carter? No, no. Cartwright! Becky Cartwright. She lives down the street from us. Do you know her?"

"No, don't think so." I looked beyond Owen to where the teenagers sat. The boy and girl hadn't spoken since they sat down. They were facing each other, thumbs flying, eyes on their phones. Ah, young love!

"Oh, well, she seems nice enough. She's divorced, lives alone."

"What were she and Becky doing?"

"I ..." He looked at the ceiling, then back at me. "I really don't know. They were out together all the time. Sometimes just the two of them; sometimes with other people, women in the neighborhood. I know they liked going up to the mountains. And then there was shopping and movies, art galleries maybe. Hell, half the time she never told me where she was going or when she'd be back, just that she would be out with the girls."

"They never invited you to go with them?"

He shook his head. "I was usually working anyway."

"Working? You sure you haven't found someone on the side?" Given his history, I didn't feel asking that was out of bounds.

"Of course not!" He sounded outraged at the suggestion. I didn't necessarily believe him. Experience had taught me that Owen was a talented liar and working had always been his favorite excuse for being out of the house.

"Are you sure?"

This time he went for sincerity. His expression softened and he leaned forward. "I've never been unfaithful to Sarah."

I could have pushed it, but why argue? "Okay, was she having problems with anybody?"

"No, nothing like that. But she was ... I don't know how to explain it. She was just acting crazy. Back in January she and Becky started going up to Blue Ridge to search for rocks. Day trips, even overnight ones."

"And they went up there to find *rocks*?"

"Yeah, rocks. There are these rocks you can find up in the mountains that have crosses formed on them. They are supposed to be lucky, like talismans or something. She found quite a few. I think she might have bought some, too. Hell, they're all over the house."

I remembered the gray stones scattered around Sarah's body. "Are they very valuable?"

He gave a weak laugh. "I don't think so. But she and Becky kept going rock hunting. In fact, they were at it again just last Friday. She didn't get home until after midnight."

"Anything else?" I looked at my watch. It was nearly 4:00 and I didn't see how my listening to Owen's complaints about his wife was helping. The police could investigate all this much better than I could.

"Well, she's been spending money like a drunken sailor."

"On what?"

"Good question." He took a swallow of his coffee. "I never used to check our bank account—just at the end of the month. But lately I've been looking at it every day. Sarah was making cash withdrawals several times a week, two or three hundred dollars at a time. When I confronted her, she wouldn't tell me where the money was going, just said she needed it."

I shrugged. "Still … that doesn't sound like enough money to warrant killing her." I drank the last of my coffee. "What happened last night?"

"Nothing. I mean, nothing I know about. I saw her at dinner. She warmed up some leftovers. Then I had to go back to the office, had a lot of work to do this weekend. She was gone when I got home."

"What time was that?"

"Ummmm… about ten, I guess. When I went to bed around midnight, she still wasn't home."

I didn't bother challenging his story about the time he supposedly spent at his office. I recalled plenty of nights when we were married that he'd claimed to be working late. "And you didn't hear anything until you got up this morning?"

"Nothing."

"Is there anything else? Anything out of the ordinary happen last week? You're sure Sarah didn't have a run-in with somebody? Was she upset about anything?"

He shook his head. "No. I know she went shopping on Tuesday because there were a bunch of bags on the bed when I got home that afternoon." He paused, thinking. "She had new tires put on her car Thursday. I made the appointment for her. And, like I already told you, she went to the mountains on Friday."

I looked around. The teenagers were still thumbing in silence. I couldn't think of anything else to ask.

"Well," I said, reaching for my purse, "you're not under arrest, so you're probably okay. What hotel are you going to?"

Ten minutes later I dropped him at a nearby Holiday Inn.

Before he closed the car door, he asked, "When will I get my car back?"

"That's up to the cops. You can always rent one, can't you?"

Driving away, I wondered if I should have been more sympathetic, but then decided I shouldn't have. More than anything else, I was annoyed that I'd gotten myself involved, trying to help a man I'd despised for years.

I pushed a button on the dash and, a moment later, music filled the car. The situation was still an uncomfortable one, but it was made a little better by Robert Earl Keen singing *Ride*. For a moment, I was tempted to follow the suggestion and do just that. But then I thought about Curtis waiting for his dinner and steered the car in the direction of the house.

SIX

AFTER SUCH A CRAZY DAY, A QUIET EVENING WAS A WELCOME thing. Nick and I talked briefly around ten.

"I won't keep you long," he told me. "You must be exhausted."

"Yeah. Long day. But things have settled down. The police released Owen and we talked some, but there still aren't any answers as to who killed Sarah." I didn't want to talk about the murder anymore. "How was your flight?"

"Long. I'm tired, but I'll perk up once I get a meal. We have dinner reservations for 7:30."

"Are you meeting with the clients tonight?" I asked. Usually he took overnight to settle in before the business began.

"Oh, no. It's just me and Frances tonight."

"I didn't know she was going with you." Frances Calvin was the chief financial officer for Buckley Construction. I'd met her a few times and come away with an impression of a gorgeous woman who was smart enough to get exactly what she wanted. She was easily the youngest executive in the company unless you counted Nick's son, Jonathan.

"I need her on site this time. There are some pretty complicated things to work out and I'd much rather she deal with them than me."

"Well, I hope you have a good dinner. As for me, I'm past thinking about food tonight. It's after ten here."

"Sleep is next on my agenda, right after eating," Nick said. "I'm still operating on Georgia time."

Just before ending the call, he said something that made my stomach drop like a roller coaster ride.

"Can't wait to get home. I'm looking forward to getting you on the bike this weekend."

Nick loved his motorcycle and had been trying to talk me into going for a ride with him for months. I'd managed to avoid it until now.

"I'm not sure … we'll have to see about that."

"Come on, Emily. Last night you said you'd try it."

And I had, under the influence of a romantic evening and several glasses of wine. But now I was sober and the thought of climbing onto the back of a motorcycle absolutely terrified me.

"Okay," I said unwillingly. "Maybe a short ride—real short. And only if the weather is good."

He chuckled. "I'll hold you to that."

I was in bed by eleven, but that impending motorcycle ride made my sleep a little restless. I kept waking up with my heart beating fast, wondering how I was going to go through with it. Curtis, on the other hand, slept soundly.

The Blount County District Attorney's Office is located in a decades-old, three-story brick building on the Marinville historic square, just two blocks away from the county's modern new court-house. At 9:00 on the first Monday in April, it was a busy place. Prosecutors rushing to get to court shared crowded hallways with their defense counterparts heading for plea meetings. Everyone was in a hurry.

I took a crowded elevator to the third floor. Although there was plenty of activity there, it was quieter. Down a long corridor that needed a coat of paint I found Annette Thibidoux in her small, neat office. An uncluttered desk, a file cabinet, and three chairs were the only furnishings. She was as striking as always, but today her long braids were pulled back at the base of her neck, she wore only a tiny amount of makeup, and her athlete's body was partially hidden by a modest navy suit. During business hours, there was no one more businesslike than Annette.

We'd been friends for a long time. After 20 years with the Blount County Police Department, I'd taken early retirement. But I soon discovered that retirement wasn't as much fun as I'd expected and had taken a job as an investigator with the DA's Office. Annette was already employed there in the same position. For several years, we were assigned to the same prosecutors. Not only had we made a good team, we'd become close friends.

Since leaving the full-time job a couple of years back, I'd con-tracted with the DA's Office as a part-time consultant and Annette was my contact. Every week or two, she assigned a few cases to me—the routine ones that the full-time investigators didn't have time for.

"I heard about Owen's wife," she said as I took a seat in a chair across the desk from her.

"Yeah. It's a mess."

"Do you think they'll charge him?"

"Hope not. We'll just have to see. I don't suppose you've heard anything here?"

She shook her head. "Nothing, but you know we don't usually get involved until they've made an arrest."

I nodded and took five folders from my briefcase.

"These are done," I said, handing them to her.

"That was quick. Any problems?" she asked.

"No, all your witnesses checked out. The investigations were by the book. They're ready for court."

She nodded and set the files to one side, stacking them carefully so that the edges lined up.

Then she looked at me and grinned. "Now to the really important business. I hope you don't have any plans for the last weekend in May."

"No, I don't think so."

"Good. Scott and I set the date!"

I rushed around the desk to hug her. Annette had played the field for a lot of years, never serious about any man. I'd been astonished, but delighted, when she'd moved in with Scott Barksdale in January. The decision took longer than it should have because of her concern about how people would react to his being white and her black.

But Scott was a determined man and he'd finally won her over, convincing her that the world today was far different from the one in which she'd grown up. Now she proudly flashed the diamond on her left hand and displayed a picture of the two of them on her desk for everyone to see.

"It won't be lavish," she said. "Just a few friends—and Mama, of course. Scott's parents died a long time ago, but his brother, Ken, will be there. Other than that, he just has a few cousins he hasn't seen in years. It'll be a simple ceremony in the back yard so that Jules and Jacques can attend."

Jules and Jacques were her two standard poodles.

"That's a wonderful idea! Just let me know what you need me to do to help."

"I will. Soon. Just give me a little time to get used to the idea that I'll be married in two months."

"I will. Your wedding is going to be a legendary party!"

"A *small* legendary party."

Before I left, she gave me six new cases. I promised to get them back to her soon.

The mail had been delivered when I got home and, sure enough, there was a letter from the HOA ordering me to have my roof cleaned. I walked out into the cul-de-sac where I had an unobstructed view of the roof. I had to admit that it didn't look good — dingy and streaked with black dirt.

"I have to have mine washed, too."

I turned, startled. I hadn't heard Marty Berkowitz, my next-door neighbor, approach from behind me.

"Oh, hey, Marty. Yeah, I got the letter."

He looked at my roof, then over at his. "I suppose they're right. They do look pretty bad. I just hate people telling me I *have* to do something."

I smiled. "I know what you mean. That's the price we pay for living here, I guess."

I was halfway back to my driveway when he asked a question.

"Have you heard anything about some neighborhood parties getting out of hand? You know, loud or boisterous or whatever." I remembered Linda's crazy sex party rumors, but I sure wasn't going to volunteer that. I didn't need to get tangled up in Marchpoint's grapevine. "No, I haven't. Why?"

He shrugged. "Oh, just something somebody was talking about at the clubhouse."

I was always amazed at the way fantastic stories flew through our neighborhood. If a woman got smacked in the face by a ball during a tennis match, by the next morning there would be whispers that she'd received that black eye in a fist fight with the mailman.

After lunch, I gave the new cases a quick review. It didn't appear Annette had given me anything out of the ordinary. I'd probably be able to knock them out in a few hours. It was something I'd leave for later in the week.

I was trying to decide between a quick trip to the supermarket or leftovers for dinner when the phone rang.

"I've been arrested, Emily. They're taking me to jail."

"You shouldn't be calling me, Owen. Call an attorney."

"I already did. Mike Bishop is going to meet us there." Bishop was one of the best criminal attorneys in the state and also one of Owen's closest friends. There was a time that we had regular dinners with him and his wife, but that was before the divorce. "The detectives are letting me make a couple of calls before we go."

"That's nice of them, but why are you calling me?"

There was a pause, then he said, "I thought maybe you'd tell Drew and Chelsea."

"Have you told them about Sarah's death?"

"Ummmm...no, not yet. I was going to call them tonight." Wonderful. Now I'd have the double pleasure of telling our son and daughter that their stepmother had been murdered and their father was under arrest for the crime.

"I hate to ask you, but I won't be able to make bail until tomorrow," Owen said, "after the first appearance. And I'd hate for them to find out from somebody else."

What could I do but agree?

I waited until after dinner to start breaking the bad news to the family. Fortified by a cold beer, my first call was to Chelsea. She lived in Greenville, South Carolina, with her husband and two children.

"Hi, Mother! How are you?" The sounds of what I thought must be a television could be heard in the background.

"I'm fine. I —"

"Just a second. Isaac, Cornelia! Turn that game down. I'm trying to talk to Grandma!" The decibel level diminished.

"So, what are you up to?" She sounded cheerful and energetic, as she almost always did. I hated to have to change that.

Chelsea took it hard, with tears and protestations of impossibility. While I knew she and Sarah had gotten along okay, she adored her father and always had. I tried to sound reassuring when I agreed that he could never be convicted, even though I wasn't convinced myself. How could I be when I had no idea what evidence they had against him?

After talking with Chelsea, I made the call I really dreaded. My mother, Marla Appling had given up her large family home several years ago and moved into an upscale independent living apartment in Greenville. It was no coincidence she lived only ten minutes away from her granddaughter. The two had been soulmates ever since Mom took Chelsea shopping at the tender age of six. They came home with numerous frilly outfits for my child, but also a new bedspread and curtains for her room.

Not only were Chelsea and my mother close, they shared misgivings about my fashion and decorating styles. I knew they loved me, but I still disappointed both of them when I'd show up at holiday dinners wearing jeans and a sweatshirt.

"Why, Emily," my mother said, "it's not Wednesday already, is it?"

I called her every Wednesday and Saturday without fail. Routine was important to her and I tried to stick to it when I could.

"No, Mom, it's Monday. But I need to tell you something."

She listened in silence as I explained that Sarah had been killed and Owen arrested.

"How tragic," she said. Then she added, with a dramatic sigh, "This would never have happened, Emily, if you'd stayed with him instead of filing for divorce. You're the first divorcee in our family, you know."

I broke in before she could launch into a "stand by your man" tirade. I'd heard it all before. "Owen asked me to look into the case for him. They may drop the charges. From what I've seen, they don't have any evidence that directly links Owen to the crime. I'll make sure and keep you in the loop."

"You have to do more than look into it, Emily," she said. "You have to prove he didn't do it! After all, he's the father of your children."

It was after ten when I called Drew—seven his time. He lived in Seattle where he did something incredibly complicated with computers that I doubted I could ever understand.

His response to the news was just what I expected. Although he was clearly shaken, he kept his composure and asked for details about the case. I told him everything I knew. He asked several more questions, just to make sure he had it all straight.

Finally, he asked, "What can I do, Mom? Do you need me to come home? I can get some time off."

"Not right now, sweetheart. There's nothing you can do here. We just have to wait and see what happens next. I'll call you when I know something."

And that's how we left it.

It was my night for phone conversations. Nick called just to tell me he was thinking of me.

"I miss you," he said.

"Miss you, too. Can't wait for you to come home. Did you have a good day?"

"Yes, I'd say so. I think we've worked out most of the details. We should be able to start the project sometime next month. And we had dinner at a Thai place downtown. I tried a couple of new things that I can't wait to introduce you to."

I wasn't thrilled about his use of the word "we" because I was pretty sure it meant Frances. And it wasn't hard to recognize that what I was feeling was old-fashioned jealousy. I was ashamed of myself. Nick had never given me any reason to doubt him. Traveling was part of his job and I was well aware that Frances was an important person in his company. I needed to get a grip on my emotions.

A minute later, we said good night. I had no reason not to believe him when he told me he loved me.

Just before bedtime, Linda called.

"You weren't asleep, were you?"

"No," I told her, "but you didn't miss it by much." I'd already checked the door locks, turned off some of the lights, and was heading for the bedroom.

"I'm sorry to call so late, but I got another card!" She sounded close to tears. "I've been thinking about it all day. And I finally decided I had to tell someone. I think I have a stalker."

"What did this one say?"

She gave a sigh. "It says 'You're as lovely as the spring blooming around you'."

"That's almost poetic, isn't it? Not exactly threatening." I sat back down. This could take a while.

I'd dislodged Curtis from my lap when I'd gotten up. He was already on his way to the bedroom when I answered the phone. Now he came to sit at my feet and stare at me reproachfully. When it was time for bed in Curtis' world, it was time for bed.

"No, I know it's not threatening, but, Emily, I just looked at the envelope again and it wasn't mailed. There's no stamp, no postmark, nothing. *Somebody put it right into my mailbox.* Someone stood on the street in front of my house and put it in my mailbox! I think the stalker lives in Marchpoint!"

It took me a good half hour to convince Linda that two greeting cards didn't constitute stalking. Finally, I announced I had to hang up.

"I'm sleepy. It's time for bed. Just lock your doors and you'll be fine."

SEVEN

TUESDAY MORNING WAS PRODUCTIVE. I WORKED THROUGH two of the new cases while Curtis lay contently on the desktop beside me. Occasionally I'd reach over and rub his head, producing a contented purr. Strange as it sounds, the action seemed to help me focus on my work. The cases weren't unusual — a motor vehicle theft and a felony shoplifting. In both instances, the thieves had been caught with the goods and the witnesses, while few, were unimpeachable. It was a good bet the defendants would enter guilty pleas long before either one went to trial.

I wasn't surprised when Owen called early that afternoon.

"I'm home," he announced. "And the cops are finished with the house."

"That was quick." I saved the document I'd been working on and shut down the computer.

"Well, preliminary hearings are held early in the day."

"Was the charge dismissed?" I asked, fearing I already knew the answer.

He sighed. "No, but I made a property bond. And at least I now understand why they arrested me. It's all circumstantial, of course, but it does look bad."

"I'm sorry, Owen. I talked to the kids last night. They're both worried and Andrew wants to come home and help."

"There's nothing he can do right now."

"Yeah, I think I convinced him to wait. But it would be a good idea if you called them both."

"I will, of course, as soon as we hang up."

"Okay," I said briskly. "Glad you're home and I really hope —"

"Wait! Emily, I still need your help. You have to look into this for me."

"You don't need *me*. You have a topnotch attorney with an office full of investigators. They'll take care of it."

"But I want you. You're the best investigator I know. Most important, you know me and you knew Sarah."

That wasn't the smartest card he could have played. "Well, I *thought* I knew you and Sarah," I couldn't help saying, "until I realized I didn't."

He pushed out a resigned breath. "Yeah, and I'm so sorry about all that happened. I really am. But what I mean is that you know us ... ummmm ... knew us, what we're really like. You, more than anybody, should realize I couldn't kill someone! Emily, I'm begging you to help me."

He was begging again. The memory of Chelsea's sobs and Andrew's stoic resignation got to me. I gave in, of course. "Okay, I'll see what I can find out. But you and I need to sit down and talk again. And this time you have to be honest with me."

He offered to come to my house, but I countered, saying I'd come to his. I didn't want Owen in the one place I'd set up for myself alone, the place where I'd found my own happiness.

Thirty minutes later, I was back on his front porch. As I waited for him to answer my knock, I glanced in a small mirror hanging to the left of the front door. My reflection stared back at me with the muted look that comes with not bothering with makeup.

The door swung open. "Emily! Come in, please."

I walked into the entryway and couldn't help glancing to the right. Sarah's body was gone, of course, as were the rock lamp, the small stones, and the wooden bowl. All that remained was a dark stain on the oak floor and a fine dusting of fingerprint powder on most of the visible surfaces.

"Yeah," Owen said, noticing my interest in the office. "It's a mess. I can't believe they just left it like this."

"They're not cleaning crews, Owen, they're crime scene techs. It's not up to them to clean up the scene."

"But look at the floor." Owen seemed more irritated by the mark on the floor than he'd been about his own arrest. "That's where… that's *Sarah's blood*, for God's sake. The stain will never come out of the hardwood."

"There are companies that specialize in this sort of thing. Bishop should know them."

We sat at one end of a dining room table that could easily accommodate ten people. Once coffee was offered and refused, we got down to my reason for being there. I pulled a pen and a small notebook from my purse.

"Okay. You said all their evidence was circumstantial. Just what did the they present this morning?"

Although they weren't required to reveal their whole case at a first appearance hearing, like the one that had been held that morning, the prosecution had to present sufficient evidence to uphold the arrest.

He seemed to wilt a little in his chair—like a balloon with a tiny air leak. "Well, you already know part of it— the fact that I was here when she was killed, that the doors were locked and there was no sign of forced entry."

"Wait a minute," I said. "You're sure the doors were locked?"

He nodded.

It didn't matter to the state, I knew. After all, Owen was *inside* the house when he found Sarah's body and called the police. He could have locked or unlocked every door in the place. But it mattered to me. I knew that all the exterior door locks in Marchpoint were deadbolts. Each one had to be opened with a key. And I didn't see that Owen had anything to gain by lying about the locks.

"Does anyone else have a key to your house?"

"I don't think so. I've never given anyone a key and I don't know why Sarah would."

"Were Sarah's keys here Sunday morning?"

He looked a bit annoyed at all the questions, but forced himself to answer in an even voice. "I don't know. I guess so. How else would she have gotten in the house?"

"Did you see them?"

He thought for a moment, then jumped up. "She always leaves her keys on the table in the foyer." He hurried out of the room and was back in less than a minute. "They're not there. The police must have taken them."

"Did they take her car?"

He shook his head. "No, it's in the garage— covered in fingerprint powder like every damn thing else in the house."

I made a note. "Then we'll have to check to see if they took the keys for some reason."

46

He was getting impatient and I couldn't blame him. The last couple of days had to be the worst in his life. I'd probably have felt worse for him if he just didn't act like such a jerk all the time.

I tried to be more understanding. "Look, I know you've been answering questions for the last 24 hours, but, if I'm going to help, I still have to ask them."

"I know. I'm sorry." He sat up a little straighter in his chair. "Ask whatever you want."

"The question about the keys is important because, if they're not here, and if the police don't have them, then the killer must. He had to have them to lock up after he left."

"Why would anybody do that?"

"I don't know. Did the police remove anything else from the house? Clothes? Towels? Could you tell if they went through your garbage?"

"What? No, nothing like that."

I nodded and made more notes.

"So what else did they present at the hearing?"

He looked uncomfortable. "Well, they talked to Charlie and Meredith—they live next door. I guess they heard us arguing Saturday night. It…uh…it was right after dinner and it got pretty loud. Sarah was completely out of control! Screaming. She smashed a vase that we bought in Asheville on our honeymoon."

"And what did you do?"

He looked embarrassed. "I guess I was shouting, too. I can't remember ever being that furious in my life. Finally, I just left."

"Where did you go?"

"Like I told you before, I went to the office."

He was lying, but we'd get back to that.

47

"What were you arguing about?"

"The money she kept spending. She wouldn't tell me where it was going. And the crazy way she's been acting …" He just shook his head.

He wasn't telling me everything. "Is that all the prosecution presented as probable cause, that the neighbors overheard an argument?"

"Well, there might have been more than one fight."

I'd have to talk to the neighbors myself if I wanted a straight answer. "What else?"

"They looked into our finances—I don't know how they did it that fast—but they did and they found out that Sarah had been taking money out of our accounts."

"You already knew that, didn't you?"

His jaw was clenched and color was flooding into his face. "I knew about the checking account, but I didn't know that she'd damn near wiped out one of our IRAs! And she took $20,000 from one of the investment accounts! There's almost $38,000 missing! What the hell was she doing?"

"You didn't know?"

"Of course not. If I had, I'd have put a stop to it. I never checked those accounts. I trust my investment guy and generally know what's in there. They send us monthly reports by email, but sometimes I don't look at those either. You know, the amounts stay pretty much the same and I don't always want to see all the little ups and downs. If you follow that stuff too closely, you'll drive yourself nuts." He shook his head. "I almost fell off my chair when they introduced that in court this morning."

"And you still don't know what she was doing with the money?"

"No idea."

"Okay. Let's try another direction. I know I asked this before, but I want you to really think about it. Did Sarah have any enemies? Anyone she'd had problems with?"

"No, nothing like that. I can't remember her ever having cross words with anybody."

I could vividly remember the cross words we'd had, but there was no point in bringing that up.

"The only person she had problems with, I guess, was me."

I thought for a minute, then asked, "Had she heard from Don lately?"

"Don? *Candler?*" He sounded incredulous. "Of course not. He's been out of the picture for years."

Don Candler was Sarah's ex-husband. I knew they'd been divorced for fifteen years or so and only had one child. It was certainly unlikely that he'd come back into her life, but stranger things have happened.

I noticed a blue pottery platter on the sideboard. It held four odd-looking stones. I stood and walked over for a better look, picking one up and turning it over in my hand. An inch and a half long, it was smooth on three sides, but there was a raised area on the fourth side that resembled a short, squat cross.

"Are these some of the rocks Sarah brought back from the mountains?"

"Yeah, she called them fairy crosses, whatever that means," he shrugged. "I don't see anything special about them. I mean, sure, they've got those formations on one side, but they're still just rocks. And if you can just pick 'em up off the ground, they can't be all that valuable, can they?"

I bounced the stone gently in my palm. "Could I take one of these with me?"

"Hell, you can take 'em all, if you want."

"No," I said, slipping it into my jeans pocket, "one's enough." I thought I might need it. "Is there anything else you think I need to know?"

He rubbed a hand over his face. "Honestly, Em, I think she was losing her mind. It wasn't just the rocks. She started wearing red. Just *red*. Everything was red — underwear, jeans, dresses, everything. She got rid of all her other clothes. It was crazy!"

"And that's not all. Did you see the front porch? She painted the ceiling blue! Why would someone do that? And she hung that stupid mirror up. Who puts a mirror on their front porch? Did she think the UPS guy needed to check his hair when he delivered a package? I swear I never knew what to expect when I came home."

"It does sound strange," I said, sitting back down at the table. "Maybe she was having some kind of mid-life crisis, but I don't see how it gives us a motive for murder. The money is where we should be looking."

"Yeah, I guess you're right."

"Did she buy anything particularly expensive?"

"No. At least nothing I know about. That's the strange thing. There was no expensive jewelry and I don't think the new clothes were from designer shops. I know some of them came from Target — the bags are still in her closet."

I nodded. The easy questions were over. Now it was time for the hard stuff.

EIGHT

"OKAY, OWEN," I SAID WITHOUT A TRACE OF SYMPATHY IN MY voice. "It's time for you to level with me."

"What do you mean? I've told you everything I can!" He threw up his hands in a gesture of innocence.

"You haven't told me who you've been seeing."

"How can you even ask that?" Eyes wide, he was the very picture of wounded outrage. "With my wife lying dead in the morgue?"

He didn't fool me. I'd seen him lie too many times. You could say I was a veteran of the Owen Christopher profession of innocence. It didn't even make me angry anymore.

I kept my voice even. "You're wasting time lying to me, Owen. And you are lying. You know I've always been able to tell."

He started to protest again, but I held up a hand to stop it. "But it's not me you have to worry about. The police will find out—if they haven't already."

He frowned and I realized he hadn't thought about that.

"And if—or I should say when—they find out, they're going to use it to build up the case they've already made against you." I held his eyes for a long, serious moment. "If you don't tell me the truth, there's no way I can help."

I could see the struggle taking place in his head. He wanted to deny everything, but common sense, and his legal training, finally convinced him that wasn't going to work. Still, he couldn't give up his virtuous persona.

"Look, Emily," he said, sincerity almost dripping from each word, "you have to understand how it's been. Sarah was so distant. We didn't have a real marriage anymore. She acted like she didn't want to have anything to do with me. She made me feel like I was just in the way. That's the only reason ..."

I didn't say anything. I wasn't going to make it easy for him.

"If things had been better at home, it would never have happened. But Jane and I were working together on the Bergman case and she was so kind to me. I mean, I just started confiding in her and one thing led to another... I'm sorry it ever happened, but it did."

I wondered if that was the same excuse he'd used to justify cheating on me with Sarah. But I reined myself in before I went too far down that road. It didn't make any difference now anyway.

"Jane who?"

He paused a beat, then said, "Carelli. Jane Carelli. She's a paralegal with the firm."

"Are you sure that you and Sarah weren't arguing about Jane on Sunday night?"

"No, no, I swear we weren't. I don't think she had any clue that I was seeing someone else. I'm telling you, she didn't care what I was doing. She was in her own world."

"Okay." I nodded. "Maybe Buddy Webster will talk to me about this. It won't hurt to call him. And I'll ask around, talk to the neighbors and that friend of Sarah's. What was her name again? Becky?"

"Cartwright," he supplied.

I made a note without comment, then put the pen in my purse. "Is there anything else I should know?"

He just shook his head.

"All right then." I got to my feet. "Let me know if there are any developments and I'll keep you up to date with what I find. Right now, it still sounds like a fairly shaky case. They may decide not to prosecute."

"But that's not good enough! I have to clear my name. And we need to find out who killed Sarah."

I didn't miss the order of importance in those statements. Owen would always be Owen.

I was home before 3:00 and felt the need of some exercise. Without even changing clothes, I took a bike ride around the neighborhood—on a bicycle not a motorcycle. Unlike Nick, this was my kind of two-wheeling. Everyone needs something to keep in shape. Riding a bike was my activity of choice.

The day was glorious, cool and sunny. I took a deep breath. The air was faintly scented with spring flowers and somewhere close someone had fired up a charcoal grill.

Another bike shot past me and I recognized the slim figure, hunched forward over the handlebars and peddling like his life depended on it, as Karl Schmidt. He lived in The Meadows and I'd heard he once competed in the Tour de France. From my vantage point, he could still have been a contender. And he kept the rest of us on our best behavior. Seeing him whiz by made me pick up my pace a little.

I passed several joggers and at least a dozen walkers. Most everyone smiled and waved, except for Leo Montgomery. He just kept his head down and put one foot in front of the other. The only unpleasant moment came when I approached the four-way stop at Marchpoint Boulevard and Golden Meadow Lane. I stopped. A car approached from the right and, as it slowed, I started across the intersection. But the car didn't stop. It kept rolling, right through the intersection, missing me by less than two feet.

I managed to stop the bike without falling, then looked behind me at the car, a white Mercedes. I expected the driver—all I could tell was that it was a gray-haired, white man—to stop, or at least send me an apologetic wave. He did neither, just kept going, leaving me straddling my bike on the side of the street, glaring after him. There weren't that many Mercedes in the neighborhood. I knew I'd see him again and, when I did, I'd make a point of telling him just what I thought of his driving.

Linda Winkler and I have a standing date for dinner every Tuesday at The Good Grain in Marinville. I arrived first, just before seven and got a table by the window. Linda, in jeans and a deep blue peasant blouse, was there within five minutes.

She dropped into a chair with a big sigh. "I was afraid I'd be late! My class ran long."

"What was it tonight? Past life exploration?"

"No, that's the first Wednesday of the month," she said, a little miffed that I couldn't keep up with her schedule. "Tonight was tarot, of course."

"Of course."

In addition to operating her shop, Linda also conducted classes there, exploring various New Age subjects. I knew about past life exploration, the meaning of auras, and tarot, but I was sure there were more subjects I hadn't heard about.

"Well, I'm glad you made it." I picked up my menu. The Good Grain is a vegetarian restaurant and one of the few places Linda could eat without worrying about encountering any sort of animal product. Their food is so good that I don't even mind the absence of meat.

Located in an old house in Marinville's historic district, the restaurant was a popular place. On weekends, tables were hard to come by, but only seven or eight were occupied that night.

We ordered dinner and a glass of wine—organic, of course. While we waited for our meal, Linda announced she had good news for me.

"When the students were practicing tonight, I did a spread of my own—for you. I asked about the outcome of your investigation." She gave me a big smile. "It looks good. You're going to discover the truth!"

"Well, that's good to know." I smiled and sipped my wine.

A minute later, one of the young wait staff placed our food on the table—a miso stir fry for Linda, mushroom and spinach fettuccini for me.

"And it gets better!" Linda said, her eyes bright with excitement. "You're in a really good place right now. Everything should go your way. The Star was prominent in the reading. It's almost like you have someone or something watching over you. Like a guardian angel."

She took a bite of her dinner and smiled blissfully. "The best stir fry ever!"

I tasted mine as well and wasn't disappointed.

"I hope your reading was right," I said. "I can use all the help I can get with Owen being arrested for Sarah's murder."

"No!"

I was surprised she hadn't already heard, the rumor mill being what it is. She must have been out of the loop somehow. So I told her everything that happened.

"At least he made bail," she said. "It must have been horrible to be locked up with all those criminals!"

I shrugged. "I'm sure it was, but he's probably represented half of them over the years. And it wouldn't surprise me if he didn't pick up some new clients while he was there."

Linda frowned. "That's not very sympathetic."

"I'm not feeling sympathetic. I spent the whole afternoon hearing about his new girlfriend and how weird Sarah has been acting lately. Of course, being married to Owen could make anyone act weird."

Linda giggled. "Well, you should know." She took a bite of broccoli, then asked, "How was she acting weird?"

I told her how distant Owen said Sarah had become and how she and her friend Becky went out all the time. "He said he didn't know where they went, and if she was simply avoiding him, I guess it doesn't matter. But she'd started taking a lot of money out of the bank and their retirement accounts. She hadn't made any big purchases that Owen knew about and he says he doesn't have a clue what she was doing with it."

Linda lifted her wine glass, drank and nodded thoughtfully. "You know, if she was unhappy and planning to leave him, she could have been stashing the money in a bank account of her own. After all, they haven't been married that long. Owen's a good attorney. She probably knew she wouldn't get much in a divorce settlement."

I just stared at her for a minute. It was easy to think of Linda as flighty and superstitious, but there was a sharp brain working under that facade. She was right. I hadn't even considered that scenario, but I did now.

If Sarah knew that Owen didn't check the accounts that often, she could have cleaned them out in a month or two and he wouldn't have been any the wiser. It wasn't a bad idea, especially if she had a good plan for hiding it. Keeping money you already have is always easier than trying to get it in a settlement.

Unfortunately, if that's what she'd been doing, it only made things look worse for Owen.

"Avoiding Owen and putting money aside for herself... none of that sounds particularly weird to me," Linda said.

I took a last bite of fettuccini and pushed the plate away. If I ate any more, I'd be miserable. Linda was still working on hers and I knew she'd finish every bit of it. For as long as I'd known her, she'd eaten like a lumberjack, but never seemed to gain an ounce. She wore a size 3 in high school and I was pretty sure that hadn't changed. Her metabolism must have been incredible.

"Oh, that's not the really weird part," I told her. "She started dressing only in red—right down to her underwear. She painted the ceiling of their front porch blue and hung a mirror by the door. And she started collecting these rocks from up in the mountains. Strange-looking little things with these cross formations on them. Owen called them... crosses... some kind of crosses. She had a lot of them."

I pulled the stone Owen had given me from my purse where I'd put it when I changed clothes. I stretched across the table to hand it to her.

Linda's face lit up. "It's a fairy cross," she said, turning it over in her hand. "And a nice one."

"Yes, that's what he called it. How did you know?"

"They're famous! I suppose you could call them good luck charms, but they're not found anywhere except in the north Georgia mountains and a few places in Europe, I think. There are a couple of legends about them.

"One is that, when the fairies learned of Christ's death, they cried and their tears fell on the rocks and the crosses were formed. Another is that the crosses appeared during the removal of the Cherokees, that they were created from their tears as they left their homeland."

She nodded her head emphatically. "The stones go along with the other things you said she was doing."

"How?"

"It sounds like she was trying to improve her luck. All those things you told me about are supposed to bring you good luck and keep evil away. They're pretty common, you know.

"The blue paint and the mirror on the porch are meant to capture any evil spirits that might try to come in the house. And wearing the same color, especially red — it's really powerful, you know — is said to attract good luck." She was still examining the stone. "But the fairy crosses. I've always thought they were something special."

She handed it back to me and I tucked it into my purse again.

"I've never heard of any of that. And I didn't even know there were such things as fairy crosses until Owen mentioned them. But I can't see how it helps. The Sarah I knew certainly wasn't superstitious, but I guess trying to buy good luck before you go into a divorce makes some kind of sense."

"Yeah, it does. But it didn't work, did it? She had just about the worst luck I ever heard of."

We turned down dessert and, while we waited for the checks, I asked if she'd gotten another card.

"Not today. Maybe I won't get any more. They're really starting to creep me out."

NINE

I CALLED OWEN WHEN I LEFT THE RESTAURANT AND SHARED Linda's idea that Sarah might be hiding money from him in anticipation of a divorce.

"Do you really think she'd do something that underhanded?"

"It's certainly worth looking into," I said. "You need to go through her stuff tonight, look any place she might have hidden something, and see if you can find information about a bank account or safe deposit box. Can you do that?"

"Yes, of course, I can. But I can't believe Sarah could be that devious."

"Maybe she wasn't. But it's something we have to check."

Nick mentioned the motorcycle trip again when we talked that evening. "The weather is going to be beautiful this weekend. I've thought about a couple of places we might go. There's Lake Oconee or Tallulah Falls. Maybe even Augusta. I hear the riverfront is really cool."

I didn't want to think about motorcycles right then and used the first excuse that came to mind. "I may be working this weekend.

This thing with Owen just gets worse and worse and there are some people I really need to talk to."

It only took a few minutes to catch him up on what I'd learned.

"I know you don't want to hear this," he said, "but you have to consider the possibility that it was Owen who killed her."

"I know, I know. It's a possibility I can't ignore, especially with Sarah raiding their investment accounts. That's a motive if I ever heard one." I took a deep breath. "The investigation will lead where it does, all I can do is follow. But I sure hope he didn't do it. The kids will be devastated if that's the way it turns out."

He didn't mention Frances and I didn't ask. His next words held all the reassurance I needed.

"Working or not, I expect you to keep Friday night open for me—all night." His deep voice, with that hint of a chuckle, sent a little tingle right through me.

"I'll be sure and do that."

I heard from Annette a little later.

"Mama drove over from Birmingham yesterday afternoon," she said. "She's really excited about the wedding—and I'm glad she is. I know she'd just about decided I'd never get married and she's so happy. But she has all these rules about what is and isn't proper."

"Well, things are so much different today than they were when she got married."

She gave a little laugh. "I know and I'm trying to keep her happy. Emily, she says I have to have at least one attendant and I just can't change her mind on that." She took a breath. "So will you be it? My attendant, I mean."

"I'd be delighted," I told her.

"Thank you." She sounded relieved, but a bit tired. "That's one thing out of the way. Now if I can just get her to see reason on a few other matters when she gets back."

"Back? Where is she?"

"She took the dogs for a walk." Her tone rose a little with frustration. "Said they needed exercise, even though it's dark outside and we have a perfectly good fenced-in yard, they need exercise!"

Annette's usual calm demeanor sounded like it had developed some cracks. And, having met Ariel Thibidoux a few times, I wasn't surprised. Annette's mother was a real force of nature who was certain to be very involved in her only child's wedding.

"Would you like to have lunch with us tomorrow?" Annette asked. "I know Mama would love to see you."

And, I thought with a touch of amusement, Annette could use some support dealing with her mother. "Sure. I'd like that."

First thing Wednesday morning, I got Becky Cartwright's number from the Marchpoint directory and called her, but there was no answer. I left a message that it was important I speak with her and hung up, then got comfortable in front of the computer. As had become his habit, Curtis stretched out on the desktop beside me. He was generally well behaved, but every once in a while, he'd reach out a paw, hook it over my arm and pull my hand to his head. That was my signal to pet him. Since it didn't happen all that often, it wasn't really disruptive.

I'd been remembering Owen saying how well I knew him and Sarah. Maybe I once did, but not anymore. So I decided to learn what I could about her the same way I'd tackle anyone else I was investigating.

Although Owen couldn't tell me what she'd been involved with during the last few months and didn't know where the money from their accounts had gone, in the cyber age it's hard to do much of anything without leaving some sort of trail. So I checked the usual websites.

After two hours, I could say with some certainty that she hadn't purchased any real estate in the metro Atlanta area nor had she been arrested in the state of Georgia. She also hadn't been named in any court proceeding or mentioned in any local news story or anywhere else I could find on the internet.

She did have a Facebook page, but aside from some pictures of herself at a bar association function with Owen that were a few months old, there was nothing there. She hadn't posted on the page since December when she'd announced they'd be spending the holidays in Aruba. She didn't have a Twitter account and she wasn't on Instagram. By eleven, I had to admit I'd struck out.

As a last resort, I called Buddy Webster and was lucky to find him at his desk.

"Hey, Emily. Twice in a week! If I didn't know better, I'd think you were inventing reasons to see me."

"I always want to see you. You know that."

"Yeah, sure. What can I do for you?"

I had to handle this delicately. I didn't want to damage my relationship with an old friend.

"Owen Christopher asked me to look into Sarah's murder for him."

I braced for an outburst, but his answer was unemotional. "Well, I can make it real easy for you. He shot his wife and he's going to prison. I don't arrest innocent people."

63

"I know that, Buddy. I'm not suggesting you didn't have sufficient reason to charge him. I know there was no forced entry. He told me about the arguments and the money she took out of their accounts. I just... well, I didn't know if there was something else."

He sighed. "Did he also tell you about his girlfriend?"

"Uh, yeah, he told me about her yesterday."

"Well, he didn't tell us. We had to find out the old-fashioned way—asking questions and following leads. But she wasn't especially hard to find. Jane Carelli. I talked to her this morning. She's a pretty little thing, even if she is awfully naive. She's convinced that Owen is in love with her. She said she hated it came about this way, but she was sure that now, with poor Sarah gone—she calls her poor Sarah—with poor Sarah gone, she and Owen would be together forever."

"Just one more thing," I asked. "Did y'all take Sarah's keys?"

"Her keys? No, why would we?"

"Just wondering."

I sat at the desk for a while, staring at the blank computer screen. There were still a few people I wanted to talk to, but if I'd been in Buddy's place—and I had been—I'd have charged Owen, too.

Lunch at the Impresso Cafe, one of the trendy new places on the square in Marinville, was always special—good food, great service and beautiful surroundings. Annette and her mother were already seated at a table near the back wall, beneath a mural of hillside houses overlooking a bright blue harbor.

Annette wore her usual conservative business attire, but Ariel appeared ready for a tropical resort. When she stood to give me a

64

welcoming hug, I saw she wore sea green palazzo pants and a flowing floral top. As usual, she looked terrific. She might have been in her early 70s, but when you looked at Ariel—tall, slender, with close-cut silver hair—you didn't think about age. All you saw was a vibrant woman, overflowing with the joy of life.

"It's lovely to see you, Emily," she said as we took our seats. "Retirement certainly agrees with you! And Annette told me you've agreed to be her matron of honor." She gave me an appraising look. "With your coloring, I think a pale peach dress would be exquisite. Not too long, of course. Mid-calf, I think, will work just fine."

I was saved from having to answer when Annette said, "Mama, we talked about this. Emily isn't buying a bridesmaid dress any more than I'm getting a wedding dress."

Ariel nodded. "Well, of course not. We don't want anything as hackneyed as a bridesmaid dress. But it has to be special, darling. *You're getting married* after all. It must be perfect."

The server approached and we ordered. While we waited for our food, Annette talked about a case she was investigating. It was no different than those we got all the time and I realized she was trying to keep the conversation away from her wedding plans.

Our food was served then and, for a few minutes, we concentrated on eating. Then Annette announced that she and Scott were planning to honeymoon in Charleston.

"We both love it. It's such a great city!"

"And very romantic," I said. "I hope you can find a hotel on the Battery."

For a while we discussed points of interest in Charleston and memories of our previous visits there. But I could sense Ariel's impatience was growing. She fidgeted with her silverware and, as soon as there was a pause in the conversation, jumped in to return to the subject on her mind.

"Who is your florist?" she asked.

Annette laughed. "We don't have a florist. Why would we? The backyard is full of flowers. You know that. You've seen them, Mama. The only thing we have to do is keep Jules and Jacques from digging in the flower beds until after the wedding."

"I didn't know you were such a gardener," I said.

"Oh, it's not me. It's Scott. That man would rather pull weeds than eat when he's hungry." She grinned. "It's really great. He does all the work and I reap the benefits."

"They do have a beautiful yard," Ariel agreed.

"Scott's even started a vegetable garden," Annette said. "He's promised me fresh tomatoes by the middle of June."

Ariel tried to focus our attention on the wedding, but Annette kept guiding the conversation to other topics. By the time we'd finished lunch, her mother was more than a bit frustrated and I knew Annette would pay for it later.

Things looked bad for Owen, but the case was completely circumstantial. His attorney should be able to convince a jury that there was reasonable doubt. And I felt like I owed it to the children to keep looking into it. Maybe I'd find something that would help.

So when I got back to Marchpoint, I drove to Blackberry Ridge, parked and started knocking on doors. Charlie and Meredith Oswald, Owen's next-door neighbors, readily let me in and steered me into a small sitting room off the foyer. They were pleasant and willing to talk, but I could see they were confused as to why I was asking questions about their neighbors.

"We saw you over there Sunday morning," Meredith said. "You know, when the police were here?" She frowned. "But aren't you Owen's ex-wife?"

The grapevine strikes again.

"Yes, I am. I used to be with the police department and now I work for the DA's office. Because I've conducted investigations before, Owen asked me to look into this for him."

"Hmmph," she said. "You're a lot nicer than I'd be to *my* ex."

Charlie reached over and squeezed her hand. "We're newly-weds," he explained. "Only been married a couple of years. But we were both divorced before and Meredith's ex-husband was a piece of work."

"He was a horse's ass," Meredith said.

There didn't seem to be anything to say to that, so I just nodded. "I know you talked to the police and told them you heard Owen and Sarah arguing Saturday night."

"Yeah," Charlie said. "There was no way *not* to hear it. It was around seven, I guess, and I was cooking some steaks on the grill."

"Charlie's steaks are the best," Meredith interjected, smiling at him.

"We had some friends over. We were sitting on the back patio when Sarah and Owen started. They were screaming something fierce. You could even hear stuff breaking. I thought they were going to kill each other." He looked suddenly stricken. "Guess I shouldn't have said that."

"Just a figure of speech," I reassured him.

"It went on for a good fifteen minutes," Meredith said. "So embarrassing. I hated our friends had to hear all that."

"Could you tell what the fight was about?"

They both shook their heads.

"Just a lot of yelling," Charlie said, "until Owen left. The car screeched off up the street. You can still see the marks on the asphalt where he burned rubber."

"Was that the first time you'd heard them arguing like that?"

They looked at each as if they were reluctant to say any more, but then Meredith nodded.

"Well, Saturday night was the worst," she said, "but it wasn't unusual to hear them fighting. They did it all the time. I can't say they seemed to be a happy couple."

The Wecks, who lived on the other side of Owen, had been in Chattanooga visiting their daughter the previous weekend. When I asked about Owen and Sarah arguing, they said they'd never heard anything.

"But then we wouldn't," Henry Weck said. "These houses are really well insulated. We don't hear much of anything when we're inside."

Finally, I walked across the street to Anna Lumpkin's house.

"Why, hello, Emily!" she said when she opened the door. "So nice to see you. Come on in."

Her foyer walls were lined with photographs of her in different business settings with various important-looking people. One showed her shaking hands with a man I thought was a former governor, but I wasn't close enough to be sure.

"Would you like a cup of tea?"

"No, thanks. I won't be here long."

Anna was a short, bird-like woman, with a cap of white hair and ramrod-straight posture. I thought she was in her late 70s, but she could have been older. I followed as she walked slowly into the kitchen. She motioned to a small table tucked into the curve of a bay window. I sat and so did she. Looking out, I could see that her lot backed up to one of the heavily-wooded areas in the neighborhood.

Anna and I weren't exactly friends, but we were friendly acquaintances. We saw each other at the clubhouse from time to time, had taken some classes together, and had played trivia at the same table once a few months before.

"Now what can I do for you, dear?"

I explained why I was asking questions.

"It's so sad, her being killed." She closed her eyes for a moment. "I can't believe it happened right here on our little street."

"Do you know if Sarah had problems with anyone?"

She shook her head. "I never heard of anything like that."

"What about her and Owen. Did they get along?"

"Oh, I really don't know. They were always pleasant enough. I never saw any problems, but, you know, we weren't close."

"So you and Sarah didn't socialize? Go shopping or to the movies or anything?"

"Goodness no. I hardly knew her except to see her in the neighborhood." She gave a little smile. "I enjoy sitting on the front porch in the evenings, just to watch the world go by. And I'd see her with her friends, coming and going. But they were all so young." She chuckled. "I don't believe I'd have been able to keep up with them."

I knew Anna had run a very successful advertising agency and been active in local politics until her retirement several years before.

It must have been difficult for her to admit there was anyone she couldn't keep up with.

She suddenly glanced at the clock on the microwave and got slowly to her feet. "Oh, goodness, it's almost three! Forgive me, Emily, but I've got to get going. Dentist appointment, you know. I'm sure he'll find something else that needs work. He always does." She sighed. "Sometimes I think it would be easier to just have them all taken out and get dentures."

As I drove home, I noticed dark clouds building up in the southwestern sky. Spring is a time of storms in Georgia and it looked like we'd be getting rain soon. I was glad I didn't have anywhere to go.

Becky Cartwright still wasn't answering her phone that evening and I wasn't really surprised. There are so many solicitors calling these days that a lot of people simply don't answer unless they recognize the number. I decided to go see her in person the next day.

TEN

To quote Snoopy, it was a dark and stormy night, and I planned to spend it appropriately. After an easy dinner of soup and corn muffins, I turned on the TV and curled up on the sofa where Curtis joined me. By eight it was fully dark and the sound of steady rainfall made me feel like I was in a safe, snug cave.

The time passed peacefully—familiar programs on the tube and a book by my side for the boring stretches and the down time during commercials. But that changed just before ten. Our local channels broke into network programing with a weather alert. A strong line of storms was moving from Alabama into Georgia, following a northeasterly path. Suddenly a banner appeared crawling across the bottom of the screen, listing the counties now under thunderstorm and tornado watches and warnings.

Even though Blount County was in one of the watch areas, the situation wasn't especially alarming. The same tableau played out several times every year. Usually the storms rained themselves out before they got to us and this one was probably not going to be any different. It was still a good 70 or 80 miles away.

While the rain continued to fall, I hadn't heard even a distant rumble of thunder. Radar showed our area was only getting rainfall, no lightening, no hail. The worst of the weather was still on the other side of Atlanta. It still wasn't a situation I could ignore, especially when the weather guy reported that there'd already been two tornado-related deaths in eastern Alabama.

My phone rang about 10:20 and I wasn't surprised to hear Linda's voice. "Are you watching TV? Do you know about the storms?"

I told her I was.

"It looks like it might really be bad."

I tried to reassure her, but I was getting a little nervous myself. How could I not be when the TV kept issuing warning after warning?

"Can I come to your house?"

"Sure."

"I'll be there in a jiffy."

Fifteen minutes later, she arrived at my door, soaked to the skin.

"You didn't walk, did you?"

"Yeah, of course. I only live six houses away. It wasn't raining this hard when I left home."

That's when I noticed the pet carrier she held in one hand and the wet, unhappy puppy inside it.

"You have a dog!"

"Yes! Isn't she precious? I got her today at the county shelter."

Twenty minutes later, Linda was sitting on the living room floor, drying the dog with one of my bath towels. Her wet clothes hung over the shower rod in the hall bath and she'd changed into a pair of my leggings and a T shirt. She was so tiny that the leggings looked like sweat pants on her and the T shirt fell below her hips.

She sneezed twice in quick succession.

"You're not catching a cold, are you?"

"I'm sure it's nothing," she said, still sniffling a little.

I brought a box of tissues from the bedroom and set them on the coffee table near her.

When Linda brought the carrier and its occupant into the house, Curtis had gone to hide behind the big plant in the corner of the room. But now he was peeking around it to watch her and the puppy.

"I named her Angel," Linda told me, "because that's just what she is."

Now that she was out of the carrier and mostly dry, I could see that the puppy had medium-length black and white fur and was larger than I first thought. In fact, if she grew into her sizable paws, she was going to be a good-sized dog.

"I didn't know you were even thinking about getting a dog."

Linda smiled. "Well, I wasn't, not until I came across the website that the shelter has."

"Oh, those sites are dangerous! I can't look at them. I want to rescue every animal I see."

"I know what you mean. I wanted to adopt *all* of them! But when I saw her picture there was just this immediate connection." She put her hand under the dog's chin. "Look at this sweet baby. Who wouldn't fall in love with that precious face? So here she is!"

On the TV screen, reporters were standing in the aftermath of tornado destruction, doing live remotes. On the radar, which showed continuously on the right side of the screen, the storm—a band of red and yellow blobs—was moving relentlessly in our direction. It was passing over north Atlanta, but didn't show any sign of losing its strength. Now, I realized, was the time to get worried. Linda was watching, too, eyes wide.

"That red part is headed straight for us!"

"Yeah, but we've had bad storms here before," I said, trying to sound more relaxed than I was. "We'll be okay. How about a glass of wine?"

So we sipped wine and watched the radar as solemn meteorologists predicted doom and destruction. The wind was picking up outside and now we could hear thunder in the distance.

Angel started panting and shaking like a leaf in a strong breeze. Her eyes darted wildly around the room. But then something remarkable happened. Curtis left his hiding place, walked straight over to the terrified puppy, and began licking her face and ears. The effect was almost magical. Angel's shaking slowed and then stopped. She slowly laid down and, although her head was still up and her ears and eyes remained alert, she stopped her frightened panting. Curtis settled in beside her, still grooming the little dog.

"Did you see that?" Linda asked.

"Yeah. I had no idea he could be so protective."

"He's a great cat!"

"I guess he is." I took a sip of wine and returned my attention to the television.

A couple of minutes later things got serious. The weatherman standing in front of the radar screen announced that a tornado was indicated. He pointed out what he said was a hook signature. I wasn't sure what that meant, but I could see that the storm was already moving northeast across Marinville, straight toward us.

"If you're in this path, you need to take cover immediately!" he said urgently. "Go to a basement or an interior room away from any windows. Do it now!"

"Oh, my God!" Linda said. "That's us!"

"Bring the dog and the carrier!" I told her. I grabbed my purse, scooped Curtis up in one arm and ran through the bedroom to the big master closet.

"In here!"

I switched on the light. Linda and the dog went in first. I followed and closed the door. We stood there unmoving for a few seconds. Then I dropped the purse and put Curtis on the floor. Standing on tiptoe, I pulled some blankets down from a shelf.

"Sit down and back up into the clothes," I told Linda, handing her a couple of the blankets. "You can put these over your head."

I got one for me, too, and joined her. Then we sat there, side by side under the blankets on the closet floor, listening to the storm rage outside.

"What if it hits the house?" Linda asked, raising her voice to be heard over the howling wind.

I could only shake my head.

She cradled Angel in her lap. Curtis meowed loudly once, but I wasn't sure if it was fear or simple annoyance at having been disturbed and put into an unfamiliar location. I pulled him closer to me. Then I fished the phone out of my purse and punched the weather app, holding it at an angle so Linda could see it, too. The small screen showed the same radar map we'd been watching on the TV. The main part of the storm was now directly over us.

Two thunderclaps, one right after the other, shook the house. The closet light went out and the screaming wind threatened to blow the house off its foundation. Linda took my hand. She squeezed it so hard I thought she'd break some bones, but I didn't pull away. I needed that contact as much as she did.

Then, suddenly, it was quiet. I looked down at the phone. It showed that the worst of the storm had passed over us. I threw the blanket off and turned on the phone's flashlight.

"Is it over?" Linda asked, emerging from under her own cover. Her hair was a wild tangle around her head. I didn't even want to think about how I looked.

"I think so." I got to my feet and shone the light around the closet.

Everything looked secure. There was still an intact ceiling above our heads. I pulled Curtis's carrier down from one of the shelves and tucked him into it before he had time to fight. Now he was really was annoyed, but I wanted him contained. There was no way to know yet if any damage had been done to the house.

"Let's leave the animals here while we check the place out," I said.

Linda slipped Angel into her carrier and we left the closet. We were following the flashlight beam through the bedroom when the lights flickered a couple of times, then came back on.

"Wow, that's a good sign, isn't it?" Linda said.

It definitely was, especially since I knew my phone was only half charged.

We took a quick walk through the house and found no damage. The TV had gone off when the electricity did, but when I picked up the remote and pushed a button, it came back on. I was amazed to see that we still had cable. The same meteorologist was calmly reporting the situation. The storm continued its march across the radar screen, but it was now several miles northeast of us and was beginning to fall apart.

"Well, that was more excitement than I expected this evening," Linda said, trying to lighten the situation.

I gave her a smile. "You could say that. We need to check out-side for damage and then make sure your house is okay, too."

I found two hooded sweatshirts in the coat closet and we pulled them on. They might not help a lot if there was another downpour, but they at least gave us the illusion of protection.

Armed with a couple of flashlights from the garage, we stepped out into the quiet night with no idea of what we might find. The air was cool and a light drizzle still fell. In the eastern sky, lightning flashed as the storm continued moving away. The thunder was now just a faint grumble.

The streetlights showed yards littered with leaves and small branches. Nothing else seemed out of place here, but the sirens in the distance indicated there were problems not too far away.

We spent a long while circling the exteriors of both our houses, dodging puddles, but finding no visible damage. Other neighbors on the street were doing the same. The mood was upbeat as you'd expect from people who'd barely avoided disaster. Everyone seemed eager to talk, comparing stories and sharing relief that our block had been spared.

Back at my place, our glasses sat undisturbed on the coffee table. "We shouldn't waste good wine," Linda said.

"I couldn't agree more."

We picked up our glasses, raised them in a wordless toast and finished our drinks. Then Linda gathered her still-wet clothes and Angel, in the carrier, and went home. I released Curtis from con-finement and tidied up the closet. Walking back through the house, I was struck by the fact that the place looked as if nothing out of the ordinary had happened.

It was almost two. I went to bed. Curtis, who I now considered a hero, curled up in his usual spot, none the worse for the evening's adventure. He was asleep before I even had my pillows arranged. I knew he sometimes got up in the middle of the night and roamed the house, but I doubted he'd leave the bed for even a minute tonight.

ELEVEN

AFTER SUCH A LATE NIGHT, I PLANNED TO SLEEP IN THURS-
day morning, but I didn't count on Linda. She sounded ready to
take on the world when she called just after eight.

"I'm so grateful that we weren't hurt last night," she said, "but
some houses up in The Arbor were damaged—really bad, I hear."

I sat up in bed and Curtis opened one eye. "Was anybody hurt?"

"I haven't heard, but I thought maybe we should drive up there
and see if anyone needs help."

Linda was not a rubber necker, eager to see the damage. I knew
she meant exactly what she said. She honestly wanted to be of as-
sistance if there were any way that she could. Linda is always ready
and willing to help anyone or anything. She volunteered for three
separate charitable organizations and was always the first to respond
to anyone in the neighborhood who'd fallen on hard times.

And her help wasn't reserved just for people. She rescued spiders
in her house, gently picking them up in a tissue and depositing
them outside. And I knew for a fact that she once found a comatose
mouse where it had been trapped in her recycling bin. She'd put on
gardening gloves and picked it up. When it twitched, she decided
that it must be dehydrated and gave it water with an eye dropper.

After it recovered a bit, she slipped the little creature under a bush in her backyard with a capful of water and a crumbled cracker.

I got out of bed. "Okay. We can do that, but give me a little while. I just got up."

"Pick you up in 30 minutes?"

"See you then."

She was true to her word and pulled into my driveway exactly half an hour later. Dressed in jeans, boots and a Wildlife Fund t-shirt, her long hair tied back with a scarf, she was ready for whatever work needed to be done.

While our street had escaped storm damage, the same couldn't be said for the rest of the subdivision. Linda drove slowly around several good-sized branches that had crashed down, blocking part of the street. A few bright blue tarps were stretched across sections of roofs and shingles littered some of the yards.

Riding up the steep hill to The Arbor, we could see that they'd been hit harder than the other two sections. A number of trees were down and the tarps were out here in force. It looked like Blackberry Ridge got the worst of it. The street was all but impassable, blocked by fire engines, police cars, and utility trucks.

"We'll have to park here," Linda said, pulling to the curb. She sneezed as we made our way down the street.

"Are you okay?"

She sniffed once. "Probably allergies. Something must have just come into bloom."

We joined other people walking down Blackberry Ridge, passing Owen's house as we went. His seemed to be unscathed, but a number of nearby homes weren't. I was shocked at the amount of damage on the block and had the chilling realization that only a mile or two separated our street from all this destruction. We'd been incredibly lucky in The Village.

Debris—shingles, branches, broken flower pots, and other things I didn't recognize—covered the street, sidewalks, and yards. A lawn chair was imbedded in a car's windshield. I was grateful that the electrical lines were underground, so at least downed wires weren't a problem. But what I saw halfway down the street took my breath away.

"Oh, my God!" Linda gasped.

An enormous pine from the woods that edged the back of the lots on the left side of the street had come down, right onto a house. One side of the structure was crushed. Huge branches covered the driveway and most of the yard.

A small knot of people were gathered on the sidewalk, solemnly watching the activity around the damaged house.

"Was anybody hurt?" Linda asked a man in running shorts.

"Don't know. They're having to cut their way into the place."

Two prison vans arrived then. In minutes, men in bright orange jumpsuits got out of the vehicles and, under the watchful eyes of the guards, began picking up debris and putting it into big trash bags.

"Isn't that Becky Cartwright's house?" a woman asked. She held a leash with a small terrier pulling on the other end.

I looked at the mailbox and realized she was right. It was Becky's place. The fronts of Marchpoint houses are all so similar that I usually have to check the numbers on the mailbox to find a particular address, even if I've been there a couple of times before.

"Has anybody seen her?" I asked.

No one had.

There didn't seem to be anything for us to do right then unless we wanted to climb up onto roofs to spread tarps. Then I spotted a familiar face down the block. Mike Carlton was standing next to his marked unit, watching the scene around him.

"I'll be right back," I told Linda, and jogged down to Carlton.

"Hey, Mike," I said. "You're spending a lot of time in March-point lately."

He smiled. "Yeah, more than I'd like." He looked around. "And this is awful."

I nodded. "Was anybody hurt?"

He looked down. "Well …"

"Oh, no. Was it Becky Cartwright?"

"Is that who lives there?" He gestured toward the tree-covered house.

"Yeah. Was she hurt?"

"I'm sorry, Em. She's dead. Looks like she was in the back bedroom when the tree came down. The roof collapsed on that whole side. The FD got here first. They were able to get a guy in there to check for casualties and he found her. But she was already gone. They won't be able to get the body out until they cut away some of the big pieces blocking the way."

"I'm so sorry," I said. "That's terrible."

He nodded. I knew he'd seen a lot of death over the years, but it never got easier. "I hope she wasn't a good friend."

I shook my head. "No, I never met her."

"Listen, Emily, we haven't made a formal ID yet and you know we can't release her name until family notification is made. So you can't tell your neighbors."

"No problem. I understand."

I walked back to where Linda waited.

"Let's go. There's nothing we can do here to help right now."

"What did he —"

"Let's go," I repeated.

We got back in her car. She made a three-point turn and drove us home.

Although Carlton warned me not to tell my neighbors, Linda was an exception. As much as she enjoyed sharing neighborhood news, I knew that, if I told her something in confidence, it wouldn't go any further.

"Becky Cartwright was killed by that tree."

"No!" She pulled the car to the curb, stopped, and looked at me with a stricken expression.

"At least they assume it's her. There's a body in the house. They're having to cut through the wreckage to get to her, so they haven't made a formal ID yet. The first people on the scene found her, but there wasn't anything they could do."

Tears filled her eyes. "Oh, the poor thing. I know how scared we were last night. Can you imagine what it must have been like for her, all alone in her house? And then when she heard the crash —" She blinked the tears away as best she could.

It was a terrible thought. "Linda, you can't tell anyone just yet. They haven't notified her family. It would be terrible if they found out from a news story or one of her neighbors calling them. So we can't say anything until it's official."

"I won't, of course, but it's just so sad."

Curtis didn't greet me when I walked in the house. I looked up and saw him in one of his usual spots, a basket on top of a kitchen cabinet. He raised his head an inch or so, then went back to sleep. I couldn't be offended. After all, late morning is siesta time. Of course, in the cat world, just about any time is siesta time.

I pulled the phone from my purse and saw that I had a voice-mail waiting. I hadn't heard the call because I'd left my purse in the car when we got out on Blackberry Ridge. I touched the screen in the appropriate places and was rewarded with Beth Engels' angry voice.

"I understand you called Buddy yesterday and asked questions about your ex's case. Let's get this clear, Emily. Neither you nor the District Attorney's Office have anything to do with our investigation. I'd think a rule follower like you would know that. You need to stay out of it. If not, I'll have to make a call. I can't imagine the DA would appreciate one of his *part-time* flunkies interfering with an active police case!"

Well, that made it clear the police wouldn't be sharing any more information with me. Poor Buddy. The voicemail was bad enough, but he must have taken a full-force hit when she learned he'd talked to me.

Word of the tornado touching down in our area had made the local news and I received a number of calls that afternoon from friends and family, checking to make sure I was okay. I was touched that people were concerned.

Between lunch and the calls, I still had plenty of time to finish reviewing the cases Annette had given me.

The six o'clock news led off with last night's storm damage. Marchpoint wasn't the only place hit. The National Weather Service had decided it had been an E2 tornado. Not the worst, but definitely bad enough. It had left a slash of destruction over a mile long. Numerous homes and businesses had been damaged or destroyed, but only one death was reported. Becky Cartwright was now identified by name and the description "elderly woman".

I reflected that, in today's media world, if Albert Einstein were killed by a tornado, the media would probably ignore his accomplishments and describe him only as "an elderly man."

After a quick dinner, I reviewed the notes I'd made on Sarah's death. One of the curious things about her recent behavior was the frequent trips she and Becky took to the north Georgia mountains. Since I couldn't ask Becky about them now, a drive to Blue Ridge might be warranted.

Nick called about seven from Salt Lake City where he was waiting out a layover.

"I'll be here another hour," he said wearily.

"Is Frances with you?" I bit my lip. Why had I asked that? What was wrong with me?

"No, she took off last night. Her part was done."

He hadn't heard about the storm, so I took a few minutes and filled him in on what had happened.

"Thank God you weren't hurt!" he said. "I wish I'd been there with you."

I laughed. "Then there would have been three of us crammed into the closet, plus the cat and the dog."

"What dog?"

When I told him about Angel, he said he couldn't wait to meet her. While he and Curtis got along well, Nick was a dog person at heart.

He told me his flight was scheduled to arrive just after midnight and I volunteered to wait up for him, but he convinced me that wasn't a good idea. It would take the better part of an hour for him to disembark and collect his baggage, and at least that much time to drive home.

"Even if there aren't any problems, I won't make it before 2:00 and I'll be beat. We'll both be better tomorrow. And after four days apart, you're going to need to be well rested."

I went to sleep with a smile on my face.

TWELVE

THE NEXT MORNING NICK AND I HAD BRUNCH AT SWANTEK'S, a local restaurant where we ate at least twice a month. It was reliably good, casual, and we knew just about everybody who worked there. Jerseys and pennants from local high schools and state universities decorated the walls. We were late for breakfast and a little early for the Friday lunch crowd. The hostess put us in a booth on the right side and when Nathan, our favorite server, came for our orders, he started writing before we had a chance to tell him what we wanted—eggs Benedict for Nick, a waffle and bacon for me. Nathan knew us well.

Feeling very content with my life, I reached over to give Nick's hand a quick squeeze. His deep blue eyes, which contrasted nicely with his dark hair and tanned skin, seemed to shine when he looked at me. And that slow half-smile still made me feel special.

"You don't look like a man who spent yesterday flying across the country," I told him.

"What can I say? Being with you just has an energizing effect on me."

"I'm really glad you're back. So tell me about your week."

He laughed. "Hey, my week was business as usual. Yours was the eventful one. Catch me up on that."

By the time we'd finished our meal, he knew everything I did about the tornado and Sarah's murder, and I'd even gotten him to tell me a little about his time in Vancouver. However, he didn't mention Frances, so I didn't either.

Over second cups of coffee, I took a deep breath and broached a dangerous subject. I was almost sure I knew what my next comments would provoke.

"You know I told you that Sarah and Becky spent a lot of time up in the Blue Ridge area. For some reason, it was important to them. I need to go up there this weekend and see if I can find out why."

His eyes lit up like it was Christmas morning. "We'll take the bike! The weather tomorrow is going to be perfect — no rain, high in the 70s. You're going to love this!"

"But…ummmm…I might need to take notes or even photos if I find something." I knew I was grasping at some pretty minuscule straws to avoid getting on that motorcycle, but it was the best I could do.

He laughed. "It's not as primitive as that. There's plenty of storage space on the bike. We could even pack enough for an overnight stay, if you want. There are some great lodges up in the mountains." He took my hand. "Come on, Emily. You'll love it, if you just give it a chance."

I doubted that, but it clearly meant a lot to him. "Okay," I said with a resigned sigh. "We'll take the bike. But let's just start with a day trip."

Nick went home to do laundry and I pulled out the vacuum

cleaner for the third time that week. I continued to be amazed at the amount of hair that comes off a cat's body. At the rate he was shedding, Curtis might be bald in another couple of months.

Linda didn't bother with the usual greetings when she called that afternoon. "Can you come down here?" she asked, her voice tight and tense. "Right now?"

"What's wrong?"

"*Now*, Emily. You have to come now."

Five minutes later I was standing in her kitchen.

"Look at it!" she said, pointing to the kitchen table.

A photograph lay beside another greeting card. I stepped closer. What I saw gave me an uneasy feeling. It was a picture of Linda walking Angel along our street.

I looked at my friend and saw she was close to tears.

"Left in the mailbox again?"

She nodded and swallowed. "No postmark; hand delivered."

The card was like the others I'd seen—floral and generic. I opened it and read the one-sentence message. *I'm so happy you have a new friend.*

"Now tell me *that's* not scary." Fear and anger took equal parts in her voice. "This creep is taking pictures of me! And he was right here on my street." Her mouth dropped open in horrified wonder. "He might even *live* here! I mean, how else could he have taken that picture without me seeing him? He might be hiding behind his curtains right now, just waiting for me to walk by so he can take more of his perverted pictures!"

Angel sat a few feet away, watching us with wide eyes.

I tried to reassure her, but I didn't like the situation either. "Maybe it's just someone who likes you and wants you to know it."

But she was having none of that. "No, it's not someone who *likes* me. It's someone who's obsessed with me! It's a stalker! And we know how that ends. We've all seen those headlines!"

"But there's no threat here," I said. "None of that 'if I can't have you, no one can' stuff."

"And that's supposed to make me feel better?"

"Well, it wouldn't hurt to report it to the police," I said. "At least that way there'll be a record, in case it … uh … really becomes a nuisance."

"Or in case the lunatic kills me?"

"No! That's not going to happen, Linda. Maybe there's some way we can figure out who's sending the cards, then we can put a stop to it. In the meantime, just keep your doors locked and don't let anyone in that you don't know. And it's good you have a dog now."

She smiled at Angel. "Yeah, she'll lick the guy to death before he gets to me."

I was getting more worried by the minute. I wasn't so much concerned about the card sender as I was her state of mind. She seemed almost desperate. "Do you want to come stay with me for a while?"

"Yeah, that would be real cozy," she said. "You, me, and Nick. Besides, that's not a solution. I can't just go somewhere and hide."

Angel went to her and Linda scooped her up in her arms. The dog gave her a few quick kisses on the chin.

"We'll figure something out," I promised.

She wasn't content with the platitudes I was handing out and I didn't blame her, but I honestly didn't know what else to do.

Nick and I watched the Braves' home opener that night—a

nice walk-off win — but we went to bed right afterwards. He was eager to get an early start the next day.

I didn't sleep well. Linda's situation really did concern me. Even though there was no reason to think the card sender was dangerous, I knew she was scared and I wanted to help her. And when I wasn't fretting about that, I was worrying about riding on a motorcycle the next day. My uneasy mind dredged up all the horrible stories I'd ever heard about motorcycle accidents. Even Nick sleeping close beside me didn't make me any less apprehensive. But morning came, as it always does, and it was time to go.

Just before eight, we stood in his garage beside the gleaming, black machine. It looked much bigger up close than it had the times I'd seen him drive by. As he'd said, there was plenty of storage space — a container on either side and another behind the passenger seat. I swallowed hard — *my seat.*

"Wow," I said, trying to cover up my fear, "it's pretty." I looked closer and saw the emblem. "And it's a Harley Davidson."

He grinned. "Yeah, an Electra Glide. Wouldn't have anything else. I've had it about a year."

"It looks brand new."

"Well, I try to keep it looking good." He reached out for my purse, opened one of the side compartments, and put it in. "Let's get your gear stored."

Then he handed me a helmet and helped me get it positioned correctly on my head, tightening the chin strap for me.

"I'll back it out first. It'll be easier for you to get on in the driveway."

I stood in the edge of the grass, helmet secure and dressed as I'd been instructed — jeans, long-sleeved denim shirt, and closed-toed shoes. I didn't like to think why my attire was important.

Once Nick was positioned where he wanted to be, he motioned for me to come to him. He was sitting astride the bike, boot-clad feet on either side of the machine, holding it in place.

"Just climb on and get comfortable. See, your feet go on these pegs on the sides."

It was a clumsy process, but I managed to get on and arranged myself as best I could in the molded seat, snug against the back rest with my feet in their appointed places. Then he started the engine. It was so loud I thought it must surely be shaking the ground around us.

"Here we go!"

We rolled smoothly out of the drive and down the street. I wrapped my arms around his waist and held on for dear life. I was sure this wasn't a good idea.

The first fifteen or twenty minutes of the ride passed in a haze of terror, but I finally realized that the motorcycle wasn't going to simply fall over. And Nick seemed to be a competent driver. He was cautious and showed no sign of wanting to do anything crazy.

My ability to breathe normally eventually returned and I gradually became aware of what was going on around me. The cool morning air rushed past us and the sun warmed my shoulders. I was happy that Nick steered us along backroads instead of venturing onto the interstate. Pastures and farm houses flew by; wildflowers and birds were plentiful, and every now and then the scent of honeysuckle or freshly turned earth reached into my helmet. It was almost pleasant.

After a while we crossed one of the many arms of Lake Lanier and, a little later, passed through the picturesque town of Dahlonega. We drove for some time on a winding highway that seemed to be cut into the side of a mountain. A rocky wall rose steeply on our left and the land dropped off sharply downhill on the right.

Finally, Nick slowed at a what looked like an old red, two-story farmhouse that a sign identified as Two Wheels of Suches—a restaurant, lodge, and campground.

"Ready for some breakfast?" he asked over his shoulder.

"Sure!" I realized I was starving. I'd been too nervous to have anything but coffee before we left the house.

There were two parking lots outside the restaurant—one for cars and trucks, and one for motorcycles. The bikes that morning outnumbered the cars four to one. In assorted colors and sizes, they gleamed in the spring sun.

We ordered at the counter from a menu posted on the wall, then ate hearty breakfasts at one of the tables.

"So what do you think of the ride so far?" Nick asked.

"It's fun!" I said, trying to put some enthusiasm into my answer.

Nick grinned. He put his hand over mine. "It'll get better once you're able to relax some."

I hoped he was right. Otherwise it was going to be a very long day.

Too soon, breakfast was over and we were back in the parking lot, putting our helmets on again. There were several people around us doing the same thing and I watched as, one by one, the bikes left the lot. I saw two other women riding as passengers and was struck by a realization—they weren't holding tightly to the men in front of them. In fact, they weren't holding onto anything. Their hands were relaxed, resting in their laps.

And at that moment I had an epiphany. I didn't need to hold onto Nick like he was a life preserver. He wasn't. Holding on to him didn't accomplish anything. If the bike went down, he was going down with it. There wasn't *anything* to hold onto on that machine. I was filled with a heady fatalism and strange sense of freedom.

So when I climbed back on behind Nick, I didn't wrap my arms tightly around him. Instead I made myself relax. I did place a hand loosely on either side of his waist, but that was just to keep contact with him, not for security. After a few miles, I was even comfortable enough to slide my phone out of my shirt pocket and take a few quick pictures as we sped along.

The idyllic scenery continued, broken here and there by isolated houses, farmland, trailer parks, and big billboards advertising everything from North Carolina casinos and local car dealerships to places you could pan for gold and gemstones. I wondered if anyone ever found gold.

We reached the small town of Blue Ridge in Fannin County just before noon. After driving from one end to the other, Nick pulled into a service station and stopped.

"Where to?" he asked.

I didn't really have a plan. There seemed to be two main streets, one on either side of the railroad track that ran through the center of town. Retail shops shared blocks with real estate agencies, law firms, and hair salons. The sidewalks were filled with people and the parked cars lining the streets displayed a variety of state tags. The spring tourist season in the North Georgia mountains was in full swing.

"Let's just park and walk," I suggested. "I'd like to go in some of these shops and try to get a feel for the place. From what Owen said,

Sarah came up here to find those fairy crosses," I looked around us, "but I don't have any idea where to start."

"Then we'll ask some questions and find out."

Nick found a place to park on a side street. We left our helmets on the bike and started down one of the main streets. I entered the first gallery/gift shop we came to. Nick was right behind me. It was called The Bluebird's Nest and was typical of shops I'd seen in other mountain towns. Pottery, paintings, jewelry, books, and t-shirts were displayed everywhere.

I checked the jewelry cases and counter tops, but didn't see any fairy crosses.

The young woman behind the register shook her head when I showed her the stone I'd brought with me. "No, we don't have anything like that. Although I think I've seen them around town before."

So we kept looking. I got the same answer in three more shops, but then we found The Rolling Stone, a little store devoted to minerals, rocks, and semi-precious stones. I thought things might be looking up.

THIRTEEN

THE ROLLING STONE WASN'T LARGE, BUT EVERY SQUARE INCH was crowded with merchandise. There were bins of brightly colored rocks and lighted display cases filled with polished stones and jewelry. Shelves lined the walls, displaying stone bowls and vases. Sitting behind a long table on the back wall was a man who couldn't have been more perfect for his surroundings if a Hollywood casting agent had hired him.

He was about our age, fit-looking, with gray hair and a big, bushy mustache. He wore jeans, boots, and a soft, plaid flannel shirt with the sleeves rolled up to his elbows. There was a cloth on the table in front of him where several brightly colored stones lay. His face was tanned and weathered, and he had a big smile for us.

"Good afternoon. How're you today?"

"Doing fine," Nick said. "You have a nice place here."

The man laughed. "Only way I could turn my hobby into something profitable." He laughed again. "Or somewhat profitable. Now what can I do for you folks?"

I pulled the fairy cross from my pocket and held it out to him. "Can you tell me anything about this?"

He took it, turned it over in his hands and nodded. "That's

staurolite, also known as a fairy cross. It's a metamorphic mineral on which crystals form—some singular, some twin and, in rare occurrences, some triples." He lifted the fairy cross I'd given him. "The ones where twin crystals form a cross, like this one, are the most collectible. Although they exist all over the world, Fannin County is one of the few places, along with Virginia and Minnesota, where they're relatively plentiful. There are also some in remote locations in Europe and Asia."

He motioned for us to follow him to one of the lighted cases near the back of the store. Inside was a display of 30 or 40 of the stones. Most were not perfect crosses, but there were raised crystals on all of them.

"Are they valuable?"

He shook his head. "Not really. Lots of folks collect them because they're supposed to bring good luck. They run from a few dollars to several hundred. The perfectly shaped crosses are the most desirable. But a lot of the other stones here in the shop," he gestured around with a hand "are much more valuable, especially the rubies and emeralds."

I pulled Sarah's Facebook page up on my phone and clicked on one of her pictures.

"Do you remember this woman?"

He smiled. "Sure. That's Sarah. She loves her fairy crosses. She's been here a lot."

"Did she have a friend with her when she came?"

"Most of the time, yeah, but I don't think I ever knew her name. Sarah usually does all the talking. And she's the one who buys the staurolite."

"Was she here last week?"

"No, not last week. I haven't seen her in a couple of months, but back in the winter she came in just about every week, buying more fairy crosses."

"Maybe she didn't want to buy them anymore and decided to go out and find her own," I suggested.

He chuckled. "People do find staurolite out in hiking country, but those trails aren't like a walk through a city park. I can't see Sarah climbing mountains or sloshing through streams, getting all hot and sweaty, can you?"

I shook my head. "No, I really can't." The Sarah I knew avoided any sort of discomfort.

He gave me a searching look. "Why are you asking about her?"

"She died."

"I'm real sorry to hear that."

"Her husband just wants to know what she's been doing."

He nodded. "We always want to know stuff like that when it's too late, don't we?" He smiled sadly. "I hope you can bring him some peace."

We wandered around Blue Ridge a little longer. Now that I knew where Sarah had been getting her fairy crosses, my reason for visiting the town was satisfied. But it was a pleasant place. With the nice weather and the tourists roaming around, there was a festival-like feeling to the place—but a subdued, well-behaved festival.

Looking up the hill behind the town where scores of houses were built, I wondered what it would be like to live in a place like this. I imagined Nick and me settling down in one of those little houses where we could look down on the pretty town and walk wherever we needed to go. It was an alluring fantasy, but one that would have to be put on hold for several years.

The drive home was a leisurely one. Nick took a different route, but it was no less bucolic. I realized, to my surprise, that I was truly enjoying the experience and wouldn't mind doing it again.

By the time we turned into the Marchpoint entrance, it was nearly dark. We topped a small hill on Marchpoint Boulevard and Nick braked hard. Blue lights flashed a block ahead of us. We approached slowly and I saw two cars in the center of the intersection. One of them had crashed into the passenger side of the other. It wasn't surprising that Marchpoint's often-ignored stop signs had claimed two more victims.

On the far side of the intersection where the patrol car was parked, several people stood speaking with an officer. I didn't recognize anyone, but the tall, young man with a blond ponytail that fell to the middle of his back was obviously not a resident.

As Nick steered carefully past the wreckage, I noticed the car that had been hit was a small SUV with North Carolina tags and the other was a white Mercedes. I thought to myself that karma can be a bitch.

Back at my place, we ate omelets and salads at the kitchen table.

"You kind of enjoyed the ride, didn't you?" Nick asked. "Come on. Confess."

"Well, maybe a little," I said reluctantly.

"I guarantee you're going to learn to love it! You might even want your own bike one of these days."

I laughed. "Now *that* is never going to happen. You can bet your life on it!"

We watched an old movie on TV and, by eleven, I was ready for bed. But Nick wanted to stay up a little longer for the local news.

"I've been out of touch for a week. Need to catch up on what's happening."

The late newscast was fairly predictable—a couple of shootings in Atlanta, some national political squabbling, and a feel-good feature about a volunteer clean up in a rundown neighborhood. No surprises there.

Then the anchorman announced, with just the right note of sadness in his voice, "And Blount County police are saying what was originally believed to be the accidental death of an elderly woman is now considered a homicide." The picture of a storm-damaged house came on the screen. About the time I recognized the place, he confirmed it. "Rebecca Mangum Cartwright was originally thought to have lost her life when a tree fell onto her Blount County home early Thursday morning. But police have now classified her death as murder."

Then the picture changed to Owen's house, obviously shot several days before when the crime scene tape was still up. "Only four days ago another murder occurred on the same street, only a few houses away." He then recapped Sarah's murder and Owen's arrest, finishing with, "Police won't comment on whether the two crimes are connected."

"What the hell is going on?" Nick exclaimed. "Two murders here in a week?"

I could only shake my head. "It doesn't make any sense. Do we have a madman going around killing people for no reason?"

Neither of us spoke the thought I knew we shared. The only way the two deaths made sense was if Owen had killed them both. After all, there was a connection between Sarah and Becky. I started to say something about that, but decided there was nothing to be gained by trying to hash it out right then.

We went to bed, once again closing an indignant Curtis out of the room. While we were both tired, we weren't so tired that we went to sleep immediately. And when I did finally drift off, I slept deeply, giving no thought to Owen or the murders.

FOURTEEN

SUNDAY WAS ONE OF THOSE DAYS I WANTED TO LAST FOREV-
er. We slept in, had a leisurely breakfast, and spent the afternoon
not doing much of anything. With a ballgame muted on TV, we
read the Sunday paper, feeling like we had all the time in the world.

There were two interruptions. Linda was bordering on frantic
when she called that morning.

"Have you heard? There have been two murders here? Do you
think there's serial killer in Marchpoint? What if it's the same mon-
ster who's been leaving cards in my mailbox?"

"Whoa! That's a wild jump to make. I sure haven't heard anything about Sarah or Becky receiving anonymous greeting cards," I
told her, pouring my second cup of coffee. "Besides, I don't think
it's a serial killer. Sarah and Becky were friends. They could have
been involved in something together or even seen something that
got them killed."

"What could they possibly be involved in? They weren't exactly criminals," she said. "From what Owen told you and what I've
heard, they just liked to go shopping together. I don't see anything
sinister about that."

"Look, we're just going to have to wait until the police sort it all out," I told her. Back in the living room, I put my cup on the coffee table and sat back down next to Nick on the sofa. He put his arm around me, pulled me close and nuzzled my neck. It made it hard to concentrate on what Linda was saying.

"Are the police going to put officers in the neighborhood?" she asked. "You know, extra patrols or something like that?"

I couldn't remember ever seeing a police car patrolling in Marchpoint, but didn't mention that. "Maybe so. And we'll figure out who's sending you the cards. Just give me a little time and keep your doors locked."

"Call me if you hear *anything*," she said before hanging up.

Nick stopped what he was doing and asked, "Was that Linda?"

I nodded.

"Did I hear right? She's worried about somebody sending her cards?"

I gave him a recap of what had been happening, finishing with the last card and the photograph she'd received Friday.

"I don't like the sound of that," he said.

"Me, either, but I don't know what we can do to find out who it is. Linda doesn't want to make a police report. She doesn't think it will do any good. And, honestly, I'm not sure it would. There haven't been any threats. I doubt it would even be assigned to a detective. After all, no crime has been committed."

He was quiet for a minute, rubbing a finger across his lips. Then he said, "There might be something we can do. Let me use your computer."

It only took Nick fifteen minutes to locate the website for a product I'd seen advertised on television.

"You install it in place of your doorbell," he explained, showing me the picture on the screen. "If someone's on your porch or rings your bell, it sends an alert to your phone and you can see them, see exactly what they're doing. You can even talk to them, from wherever you are."

"It sounds like a great thing to have, but this guy hasn't come to her door, just to the mailbox."

"But that's the beauty of it! I thought I'd heard there were different settings. It only took me a minute to check." He clicked the mouse and the screen changed. "See? You can set it to be triggered by movement as far away as the street. So whenever anyone is at her mailbox, it'll send a picture to her phone."

I nodded, then a thought occurred to me. "But half the neighborhood is out walking all day. Won't she get a bunch of pictures she doesn't want?"

A frown creased his forehead for a moment, then cleared. "Yeah, I guess so. But don't you think she'd be willing to go through that for a few days to find the one person putting things in her mailbox?"

I had to agree that she would.

"And after she discovers who it is, she can change the setting to only the area near her doorbell."

"It's a great idea."

"Then that's settled." He turned back to the computer. "I'm going to order one for her with quick delivery. I can install it as soon as I get back from Birmingham." His fingers began moving across the keyboard. "And while I'm doing that, I'll get one for you, too. Can't be too safe, can we?"

Was there any doubt about why I loved this man?

He looked over his shoulder at me. "Why don't you call Linda back and tell her? It might make her feel better."

And it did. I could hear the relief in her voice. "That's fantastic! We're going to catch this guy in the act!"

"Nick said he'd install it for you when he gets back from Birmingham, Thursday or Friday."

"Tell him I appreciate it so much. Of course, I'll have to be extra vigilant until then."

Owen had heard the news about Becky Cartwright and called just after noon.

"This has to mean they'll drop the charges against me," he said. He sounded so sure of himself that I hated to burst his bubble.

"Not necessarily. After all, Becky and Sarah were friends. It would be quite a coincidence if there were two unrelated killings on the same block in less than a week. The police just might believe you killed them both."

"But that's what I'm saying. It can't be a coincidence! Even if they think I killed Sarah, I sure had no cause to hurt Becky. I hardly knew the woman."

I didn't have an answer for him and just wanted to get off the phone. "We'll just have to see what happens."

"I know you've been asking around, Emily, and I appreciate that. Have you found out anything?"

"No. Sorry, I haven't." I glanced at Nick. "Listen, we'll talk tomorrow. Maybe there'll be some news by then."

With that, we ended the call and I got back to my day. I wanted to spend as much time with Nick as I could since he was leaving town again.

"At least it's only for a few days this time," he said, when I told him I'd miss him. "And I'm just going to Birmingham. An easy drive."

"Is Frances going with you this time?"

He gave me a puzzled look. "No. Why would she?"

"Just wondered."

"But I'm glad you brought her up."

"Really?" I wasn't sure I was comfortable with where this was going. Had he picked up on my jealousy? "Why?"

"I'd like to invite her to dinner with us some time soon. Maybe you could make your Brunswick stew and I'll smoke some ribs. We could give her a genuine southern dinner. Poor thing. She's from New Jersey; doesn't know what real barbecue is."

"Sounds like you got to know her pretty well on your trip."

He nodded. "I did. Of course, I've known her for a couple of years, ever since she started with the company. But only as a business associate. This week I learned a lot about the person she is."

"Hmmm." I was fighting to keep myself in check. Just because he got to know the woman better on the trip didn't mean there was anything to get upset about.

"Yeah, she's funny, and really smart."

I could feel the heat rising in my chest.

"And I think she'd be perfect for Jonathan."

For a couple of seconds, it was like he was speaking a foreign language. What he said didn't make any sense. Then it did. "Jonathan? Your son?"

"Oh, yeah, he'd come to dinner, too. That way maybe he'd get to know her like I have — away from the office. You know, he hasn't had a serious relationship in over a year, ever since he and Amanda broke up. It's time he tried again."

All I could do was smile. I didn't tell him how foolish I felt.

"So, what do you think?" He asked a little impatiently.

"Oh," I said, coming back to the conversation. "I think it's a terrific idea." I grinned at him. "Although I never pictured you as a matchmaker."

He looked a little embarrassed. "Well, he is my son."

We walked across the street to Nick's house just before six. While I got busy making us a drink, he went outside to get the charcoal started in the grill. I took the drinks out and we sat on the patio, enjoying the evening.

Jeffrey Smith, Nick's next-door neighbor, stepped out into his back yard to fill his bird feeder. When he saw us, he waved and walked over.

"Afternoon, folks." He was a big man who almost always had a smile on his face. "Going to barbecue some steaks?"

Nick smiled. "Yes, we've got some nice ribeyes ready to grill."

"Sounds good. I might just have to join you."

"You're welcome to. They're big steaks. Plenty to go around."

Jeffrey laughed. "Any other time, I'd take you up on the offer, but Katie's got lasagna in the oven. And her lasagna is the best in the world."

After his neighbor went back inside, Nick said with a grin, "See what I was saying about giving Frances a real southern meal? It's important to educate the transplants. Jeff and Katie moved from Pennsylvania to Georgia over 10 years ago and he still thinks cooking out on a grill is barbecuing."

I smiled. Southerners know that barbecuing requires hours of smoking meat over a low fire. "It's a regional thing. You can't correct it, so you shouldn't even try. Lord knows what people up north would think of *our* language if we moved there."

He shuddered in mock horror. "Don't even suggest such a thing!"

The steaks were delicious and, as Nick promised, very large. Along with the vegetables he'd grilled alongside of them, I ended up taking half of my meal home for Monday's dinner.

Nick would be sleeping at his place that night. He wanted to miss the worst of the Atlanta morning traffic and that meant leaving by six. So we said our goodnights early.

"I'll call you tomorrow night," he said after our last kiss.

"Travel safe."

The phone woke me just after seven.

"Emily? It's Mike Bishop."

In my half-awake state, it took me a few seconds to place him as Owen's attorney. "Uh, yeah, Mike. What can I do for you?"

"I'm calling for Owen. He wanted you to know he's been arrested again."

"Wait. What? He already made bond."

Bishop sighed. "That was for Sarah's murder. Early this morning they charged him with Rebecca Cartwright's death. This time — two murder charges in less than a week — I doubt I'll be able to get a bond set for him."

That definitely woke me up. "I knew the police decided Becky was murdered, but what do they have that connects her to Owen? I mean, other than she lived on the same block?"

"Well, I guess it won't hurt to tell you. The cops sure aren't acting like it's a secret. She didn't die during the storm. The ME set her time of death around the same as Sarah's." He paused for a moment. "And, I don't know how to explain this away yet, they found pieces of that pink salt lamp in the soles of Becky's shoes. They told Owen that when they arrested him."

I was slow processing that information. "But—do they think they were both killed at Owen's house? And how did Becky's body get back to her place? I mean, if he was going to hide one body, why not hide two? Wouldn't someone have seen him walking down the street carrying a corpse —"

"Emily, Emily!" he said, breaking into my rambling. "I don't know. I haven't talked to the police or the DA yet. You know I'll do everything I can for him, but it doesn't look good right now." His voice became more businesslike. "Anyway, the reason I'm calling is that he wants you to let the kids know."

Of course he did. "Okay. And, Mike, thanks for letting me know."

I decided to call Chelsea and Drew later in the day. Having one person in the family wake up to the bad news was enough. It could wait a while.

For the second time in a week I was up before sunrise. After breakfast, I paid some bills and took care of some routine house-keeping. The cases I'd vetted for Annette were sitting on my desk. There was nothing complicated or problematic in any of them that required a face to face meeting. I could have emailed them in, but getting out of the house appealed to me and I decided to take them to her in person.

She could catch me up on all the wedding plans and maybe she'd heard more than I had about the case against Owen.

FIFTEEN

I've known Annette Thibidoux for a good twenty years and always considered her to be the coolest, most in control person I ever met. But the Annette I found in her office that afternoon didn't fit that description in any way. Her desk was a mess, with random papers covering the surface. As a "place for everything and everything in its place" kind of person, this was a first for her. And she was on her feet, pacing in the limited space between her desk and the window. She looked like she didn't know what to do with herself. She turned to face me when I entered the room.

"My mother is driving me insane!" she announced. "Really. The woman is driving me insane! I can't get any work done. I can't even plan for the wedding. I can't concentrate on anything!"

"What is she doing?" I asked, handing her my reports. "Is she still staying with you?"

She tossed the reports on top of one of the paper piles. "No. She drove home Saturday. She couldn't miss church yesterday. She's the choir director, you know.

"But she keeps calling me. Four times so far today! I can't get any work done for the interruptions. She's taking this whole mother of the bride thing way too seriously."

I smiled and sat down. As I'd hoped, she followed my lead and took the chair behind her desk.

"Well, she's excited about the wedding."

"That's putting it mildly. She's like this big, uncontrollable ball of energy, full of questions and worries and demands! Her biggest concern now is that we've planned the wedding for Memorial Day weekend."

"What difference does that make?"

She gave several quick nods of her head. "That was my question. And it seems that the best caterers are already booked solid for the holiday weekend."

"I didn't know you were having the wedding catered."

"We're not," she said wearily. "I've been trying to convince Mama of that for two days. And then this morning she wanted to know which band we'd hired for the reception."

"Recep —"

She held up a hand to stop the question. "There *is* no reception! There is no music! There is no caterer!" She took a shaky breath to calm herself. "There's nothing that my mother expects a wedding to be. And she's very upset about that. She believes we're doing it all wrong."

I could empathize with trying to keep a demanding mother happy. "Doesn't she understand that this is what you and Scott want? You've said all along you were going to have a small ceremony with no frills."

"Believe me, I've tried to explain that. Every time I think I've settled all her concerns, she comes up with something else."

"Can I help?"

She smiled. "Actually, you can. If you'd make some of your wonderful potato salad for our non-reception, it would be great. We're going to get a ham, the spiral-sliced kind with honey. The potato salad will go great with that."

"I'd love to. What else do you need?"

"Nothing that I know of right now, but that could change." She gave a tired laugh. "After all, the wedding's still a month off. Who knows what else she may come up with?" She tapped a finger on the reports I'd brought. "Anything in there I should know about?"

"Everything's pretty straightforward. One of the witnesses in the Johnston case has a record for shoplifting fifteen years ago, but I can't see how that could affect his testimony. It's not like he's a character witness. Otherwise, everything was normal."

She nodded. "Thanks, Emily."

I had planned to ask if she knew anything about Owen's case, but before I could broach the subject, her phone rang. She answered and then rolled her eyes.

"No, Mama, we don't need a punch bowl. Why? Because we're not serving punch, that's why."

I gave her a wave and slipped out. The question could wait.

I killed a couple of hours going over my notes on Owen's case again, but there just wasn't anything to follow up on. I warmed up the steak and vegetables that were left over from last night's dinner. They'd have been better served with Nick's company.

After that, I couldn't put it off any longer and called the kids. They were upset, of course, by the news of their father's second arrest. Chelsea cried again and, this time, I couldn't talk Andrew out of coming to Georgia.

"There's really nothing you can do right now," I told him.

"It doesn't matter. That's where I need to be," he said, "There are a few things I have to wrap up here, but I'll be home Wednesday. Thursday at the latest."

The evening was quiet after that although Linda called, still upset about what she insisted on calling her stalker.

"Any more cards?" I asked.

"No, thank God. When did Nick say he could put in that camera?"

"He's supposed to be home Wednesday or Thursday, if the trip goes well. I'm sure he'll get it installed as soon as he can."

"I hope it's soon. And I can't believe the police aren't doing anything about the murders!"

"Linda, they believe they've already found the killer and have him in jail."

"I know. I ... I heard they arrested Owen again. But what if it's not him?" She waited a moment, then asked, "Do you think it was Owen?"

"No, I don't," I said and was surprised to discover that I believed what I was saying. "I suppose anyone could kill in a rage, but I can't accept that Owen murdered Becky in cold blood. It's her death that makes me sure he's not the killer. Their whole case is circumstantial. I'm going to keep investigating it. There has to be another explanation."

I heard her blow her nose and I took the opportunity to change the subject. "Have you made that doctor's appointment yet?"

"No, I've been drinking peppermint tea with elderflower honey. That should have helped, but it hasn't. So today I bought some allergy medicine. Maybe that'll do the trick. I'm really tired of sneezing and sniffling."

I told her I'd see her the next afternoon for dinner and we said goodnight. Then I called Nick in Birmingham just to hear his voice. He was expecting to be home sometime Wednesday afternoon.

"Maybe we'll have dinner at one of the places on the lake," he suggested.

"Can't think of anything I'd like better."

I spent the next hour on the sofa with Curtis and a book. I'd turned on some music, soft rock tonight. After a while I picked up my phone and paged through the pictures I'd taken on Saturday, reliving the pleasant day we'd had. There were several shots of Nick in downtown Blue Ridge, looking happy and handsome, and I marveled again at my good fortune in finding such a wonderful man.

The rest were those I'd snapped during the ride. Given my position on the back of the bike, some were shaky and none were especially well composed, but I had managed to capture the rolling hills and the mountains beyond. I was enjoying looking at the green pastures and small farms again when something at the top of one of the frames caught my attention. It was a roadside billboard. I couldn't quite make out the message, but when I enlarged the photo, I could read it just fine.

I sat still for a minute, staring at the picture. The billboard advertised a casino in North Carolina. I knew there were several in that area operated by the Eastern Cherokee tribes. While I'd never been there, a lot of my friends had. And that's when things fell into place.

Sarah and Becky had regularly driven to Blue Ridge. There was nothing to stop them from traveling a little farther north. And if Sarah had gotten heavily involved in gambling, everything else suddenly made sense—the out of town trips, the missing money, and her desperate search for good luck.

While a trip to Cherokee might be necessary sometime soon,

a conversation with Owen was the first thing I needed. I was sure Mike Bishop could arrange for me to visit him in jail. I set the alarm for 7:30 so that I could get an early start and went to bed.

A loud crash woke me a couple of hours later. I'm not usually nervous about intruders, but Linda's talk about killers breaking into houses must have made an impression on me. I opened the bedside table as quietly as possible and removed a small revolver. Then, as silently as I could, I slipped from the bed. Barefoot, I crept down the hallway and stopped at the living room door, where I stood absolutely still and listened for a long minute. I couldn't hear anything except my own breathing.

I reached along the living room wall to the switch plate, flipped on the overhead light, and stepped into the room, ready for whatever might be there. There was no sign of an intruder, but a glass-based lamp lay broken on the floor. The space the lamp had recently occupied on an end table now held a large tabby cat.

Curtis licked his paw, smoothed it over his face, and looked at me as if he had no idea how the accident had happened.

"Damn it, Curtis!"

I made a quick survey of the rest of the house, but there was, of course, no intruder, just a cat who believed every surface in the house belonged to him.

Not wanting to leave the mess for the morning, I got a broom and dustpan and cleaned up the debris, being careful not to step on a piece of broken glass. While I worked, I glared at Curtis several times, but he didn't seem to notice. When I was done, he followed me back to the bedroom and claimed his usual spot.

It was when I was reaching to turn off the light that I realized I'd just found another piece of the puzzle.

SIXTEEN

AS IT TURNED OUT, THERE WAS NO NEED FOR ME TO GET UP as early as I did. It was after ten before I got in touch with Mike Bishop. I asked if he could call the jail and set up a meeting with Owen for me.

"You're too late. He made bond this morning. The judge put him on house arrest, with an ankle monitor." He chuckled. "That's what happens when you have a crackerjack defense attorney."

"Evidently," I said with a smile. "I didn't realize you were that influential."

He sobered. "Well, if I have to admit it, it was probably Owen's reputation and not my skill that convinced the judge."

"So he's at home?"

"Yeah. He better be. If he strays more than 100 yards from his house, they'll send deputies out to find him. And then he'll sit in jail until his trial."

"Okay. Thanks, Mike. I'll call him there."

And I did. Owen answered on the second ring.

"We need to talk," I told him.

"Go ahead."

"No. We need to talk face to face. Can I come over?"

"Sure. It's not like I'm busy."

I drove to Blackberry Ridge and parked in front of Owen's house. As I got out of the car, I noticed Anna Lumpkin sitting on her front porch again. She gave me a sweet smile and waved. I waved back, thinking how uneventful her life must be if watching the world go by on Blackberry Ridge was her primary form of entertainment.

Owen had obviously been home long enough to shower and shave. He looked fresh and comfortable in khakis and a yellow polo shirt.

"Want some coffee?" he asked. "You wouldn't believe what they consider coffee in the county jail."

"No, thanks," I said. I wasn't in the mood for friendly conversation. "We have to talk."

He gestured to the living room sofa. I sat, sinking into the puffy cushions, and he took a chair opposite me.

"Go ahead."

"You said you were here when Sarah was killed, right? And didn't hear anything?" I asked.

"I already told you —"

I stopped him. "Don't bother. I know you lied about that. You could never have slept through the noise of that lamp crashing to the floor. There's no rug in the office. It was a big rock shattering on a hardwood floor." After last night's destruction, I knew how just how loud it would have been. Even though this his house was larger than mine, I was familiar with the floor plan. Owen's bedroom backed up to the office. He would have had to hear the crash.

He still wanted to convince me I was wrong. I could see it in his face, but then he changed his mind. "You're right. I wasn't here. I was with Jane. It was after six in the morning when I got home."

I couldn't believe he'd been so stupid. "Why the hell didn't you tell the police that?"

He shook his head, eyes down. "What good would it have done? I could tell Sarah hadn't been dead long. You know how imprecise time of death can be. An hour or two wouldn't have made that much difference."

"You don't know that!" I said. "Instead of telling the truth, you made up that story about being here and not hearing anything when she was killed. No wonder they arrested you! And it was all because you didn't want to sully your sterling reputation by admitting to having an affair, wasn't it? And it didn't matter! The police found out about it the very next day!"

He nodded. "Yeah. I don't know how they found out, but they talked to Jane right after I was arrested."

"So you just made it worse for yourself by lying. And once you're on record with a lie, it's almost impossible to change the story and make them believe you're telling the truth."

He didn't have anything to say and there was nothing we could do about it now.

"Were you also lying about the doors being locked? Were they locked when you got home."

"Yes, that was true. I had to unlock the garage door when I came in. And after I found Sarah … while I was waiting for the police to get here, I checked the other doors. I thought there must have been a break in, but they were locked, too."

It was time to move on to my main reason for being there.

"I'd like to see your credit card statements, actually Sarah's credit card statements."

He wanted to ask why, but didn't. "Sure." He stood up. "Everything's in the office."

I knew that Owen was a meticulous record keeper and he demanded the same from his wife.

I followed him into the room where Sarah had been killed, trying to ignore the stain where her blood had flowed onto the floor. To the left was a small desk and a two-drawer wooden file cabinet. Owen pulled open the top drawer.

"Everything should be there. The file you want is Credit Cards/Sarah. There are folders for the last five years."

He moved to one side as I stepped up and pulled out two folders, for last year and this one.

"This may take a while," I said, dropping the folders on the desk and pulling out the chair.

He took the hint. "I'll wait for you in the other room."

Sarah had three credit cards and used them all frequently. I sorted them first by type—Visa, MasterCard and American Express—then put them in chronological order.

It took a while to get everything organized, but a pattern eventually began to emerge. In November, Sarah had charged $60 at The Rolling Stone in Blue Ridge and she'd gassed up twice in the same town. In December, she'd charged an another $58 at the rock shop. But the week before Christmas she'd fueled her car in Cherokee, North Carolina, and had eaten at a restaurant there. The January statements listed two more Rolling Stone charges and more gas and food purchases in the mountains—two in Georgia and a few in North Carolina.

Everything else in January was local—restaurants, nail and hair salons, gas stations, and department stores. But in February, I found a Visa charge for one night's stay at a hotel in Cherokee. And there were similar charges there in the following three weeks.

Owen was still in the living room where a news channel droned away on the TV.

"You done?" He started to get up.

"No, not quite yet." He slumped back in the chair. "You're right about the record keeping. Everything's there, except the bills for March. Have they come yet?"

He got up with a sigh. "Yeah, I'm sure some of them have."

A pile of unopened envelopes lay on the console table near the front door. Owen picked them up, rifled through them, then handed three to me.

"Here you go. You want to see the rest of 'em? There are a lot of bills here."

"No. Just her credit cards."

Back in the office, I looked over the most recent statements, but didn't find any more charges from Blue Ridge or anywhere up that way. My theory was shaken a little. I'd been sure that Sarah was spending all that money gambling in the casinos around Cherokee. The seemingly weird purchases of fairy crosses, mirrors for the front porch, and clothes of the same color supported my idea that she was trying to buy good luck for her gambling. And, up until now, her credit card spending seemed to support that supposition.

But the travel appeared to have stopped around the first of March. Had she quit gambling? It was hard to believe that someone who'd burned her way through thousands of dollars had simply stopped. Maybe she was afraid Owen was getting suspicious and started operating on a strictly cash basis.

I set the current bills to one side, gathered up the rest, and replaced the folders in the cabinet. As I was doing so, I noticed a file in the front of the drawer labeled Auto Expenses.

I remembered Owen saying Sarah had gotten new tires on her car a few days before she was killed. A quick look in that folder produced a receipt for the tires. I pulled it out and took it with me to the living room.

"Owen, have you driven Sarah's car since she was killed?"

"No. No reason to."

"I need to see it. And I need the keys."

"I told you the police took them."

"I asked and Buddy Webster said they didn't. I think the killer must have taken them. But you must have a second set. Everyone does."

He frowned for a bit, then got to his feet. "I think she kept extra keys in a basket in the kitchen."

"Well, let's look."

He found the basket in a drawer, located the spare key and led the way to the garage.

The little silver BMW was parked beside Owen's SUV. He opened the door on the driver's side, then cursed.

"See what I mean? That damned fingerprint powder is all over everything."

It was true. Traces of black powder were everywhere, including the white leather seats.

"Would you please get in and start it?" I asked.

"I don't want to sit in that mess!"

I sure wasn't going to sit in it. "Do you want me to keep looking into this or not?"

121

He only hesitated for a moment. "Oh, all right. Goddamn it!" He slid into the driver's seat and started the car.

I waited for the dash display to come up, then leaned my head in to look at it. Then I glanced down at the mileage reading printed on the receipt. The car had been driven only 23 miles since the new tires were put on.

"Okay. You can turn it off now."

He did, got out and used a hand to brush off the seat of his pants. Then he looked at his black-streaked palm in disgust. "Just what did that accomplish?"

I took a deep breath. It was time to let him know what was going on. "I think I've figured some things out. Let's go back inside."

"I have to change first," he said disgustedly. "I'm not ruining the furniture with this stuff."

I waited for what seemed like longer than it should have taken. When he returned to the living room, his face was flushed and he looked angry.

"Do you know how hard it is to change your pants wearing an ankle monitor? It's like training to be a contortionist."

"Just sit down. There are some things I have to tell you."

SEVENTEEN

Owen was getting irritated. Lips pressed in a tight line, he dropped into his chair. He'd never been the most patient of men and didn't like being told what to do. I'd been in his home for nearly an hour, looking through his records and making demands, and hadn't shared anything with him. Now I was ordering him to sit down so we could talk. I was surprised he'd held his temper so long and chalked it up to the fact that I was the only person around actively trying to clear him of murder.

"I think I've figured out what Sarah was spending all that money on."

That piqued his interest. "Really? What?"

"She was gambling."

"Gambling? On what? You mean like with a bookie?"

"No. I think she was going up to the casinos in the mountains, probably with Becky Cartwright, and maybe some others. You did say that sometimes other women from the neighborhood went out with them, didn't you? Do you know their names?"

"No, I don't—wait, one was Miranda, I think that's her name. Sarah met her at the clubhouse. Playing bridge, maybe? And I think she mentioned a Carol or a Carolyn or something like that." He shrugged. "But, like I told you, the only friend of Sarah's I met was Becky."

I made some notes. "Okay. Well, from the credit card statements, she went to Cherokee at least twice in December and just about every week in January. And in February, she stayed up there overnight three times.

"Cherokee? North Carolina?"

"Yes, looks like she was a regular visitor. But something changed in March. There were no charges for gas or hotels there last month. She could have started paying cash for everything or maybe someone else, like Becky, did the driving last month. Or she just stopped going."

He rubbed a hand over his face and head, leaving spikes of hair sticking up in several places. "I don't know. The Sarah I knew never had any interest in gambling. Isn't it possible she was having an affair? They might have wanted to go out of state to keep everything discreet. I think going from a few hotel rooms and gas charges to out of control gambling is a quite a stretch."

I slowed down and tried to explain what had led me to my deduction. "It was her behavior. The rocks and everything else. I consulted ... uh ... an expert in the field of superstition." I almost smiled, thinking how proud Linda would be with that designation. "Everything Sarah did was designed to bring herself good luck. The rocks, the ones called fairy crosses, are only found in a few places in the world. Blue Ridge, Georgia is one of them. And the legends surrounding them promise good fortune to people who have them."

He nodded, but didn't seem convinced.

"I know Sarah told you she went out searching for rocks, but that wasn't quite true. She bought them from a little shop in Blue Ridge. Her credit card bills show that she spent nearly $400 on them over two or three months."

He sat forward in his chair. "That much money on *rocks*?"

"Afraid so."

"What about the other crazy things she was doing?"

"Wearing the same color all the time, especially red, is another way to attract good luck. Now painting the porch ceiling blue and hanging a mirror near the door, that's different. Those things are supposed to keep evil spirits out of the house."

He wasn't able to sit calmly any longer. He jumped to his feet and paced around the room. "Evil spirits? Really, evil spirits? For Christ's sake, was she having witches cast spells for her, too? What the hell happened to her? Sarah was an educated, sensible woman. All this... I think I was right in the first place. She was losing her mind."

He stalked into the kitchen and got a beer from the fridge. He held the can up to me with a questioning look and I shook my head no. He opened it and came back to sit across from me.

After taking a deep drink, he asked, "Honestly, Emily, do you think she could have been sick? Some kind of mental thing, maybe? I've heard that brain tumors make people act strange. Or maybe it was dementia?"

"I don't know, Owen. Did she have any other symptoms?"

"Not that I noticed."

"Well, I've never heard of dementia taking the form of compulsive gambling, but I guess it's possible. Do you know if she'd ever gambled before? Gone to a casino or a racetrack?"

"Not that I know of. We certainly never did anything like that."

I shrugged. "Well, I guess it's possible that she and her friends went up to Cherokee in November or December on a lark and she just loved it. You know, gambling addiction is a real thing."

"Yeah, I know. I once had a client with a gambling problem. We used that addiction as a defense. We won, too. But does it come on suddenly when someone is nearly 50? And then they just stop after a few months?"

I could only shake my head. "I don't know enough about it to say what is and isn't normal." I looked down at the receipt for the tires I was still holding. "She got new tires on Thursday. The receipt's right here. And you told me she went to the mountains the next day, right?"

"Yeah. That's what she said."

"Did they take Becky's car?"

He thought for a minute. "No. I remember Sarah saying Becky's car was in the shop. She needed some big repair—axle replacement, maybe? And they were waiting on the parts. Anyhow, Sarah said she was going to drive. She even said she was glad she had new tires on the car because it would make her feel safer."

"What time did they leave?"

"I don't know. Sometime in the afternoon, I guess. I was at work."

"Were you here when they got back?"

He took a breath, probably to frame a new lie.

"No, don't tell me. You were 'working' that night, too."

He didn't say anything, just rubbed the condensation from the beer can with his thumb.

I looked at the receipt again. "Well, if they went to the mountains, Sarah didn't drive her car. That's why I wanted to look at the speedometer. She only put 23 miles on the car after she got the new tires Thursday."

He looked completely deflated now. "How could I have been married to her and not known anything about her?"

I bit my lip to keep from making a snippy comment, then said, "Just one more thing. Did Sarah tell you what her plans were for Saturday night."

He just shook his head.

"I know you had an argument —"

"That's putting it mildly."

"And you left, I know. But before that, did she give you any idea where she was going?"

"No. There was nothing."

"Well, she must have been going someplace special."

He frowned. "Why do you say that?"

"The way she was dressed."

He frowned. "I didn't even notice. When I found her, you know, lying there..." He shook his head sadly. "All I saw was the blood and that she was ... gone."

I couldn't fault him for that. "I understand. But she was wearing what looked like a cocktail dress and heels. You don't wear something like that to go to the movies. So she must have gone somewhere special that night."

I left him sitting in his chair, trying to figure things out. I wished I had the answers.

Linda was much more in touch with people in the neighborhood than I was so I called her when I got home.

"Do you know someone in Marchpoint named Miranda? Owen said that Sarah met her playing bridge and this Miranda went with her and Becky sometimes on their outings. There was someone else named Carol or Carolyn, but he wasn't sure either of those names was right."

"Well, there are a bunch of Carols and Carolyns in the neighborhood. But I only know one Miranda. Miranda Overstreet."

"Where does she live?"

"In The Meadows, I think, but I'm not sure. I do know one thing—she plays a lot of bridge. Several times a week, I think."

The Marchpoint clubhouse hosted card games, dominos, and mahjong just about every day of the week.

"And she likes to exercise early in the mornings," Linda said. "She's always in the gym when I go down for water aerobics at 8:30."

I thanked her for the information and told her I'd pick her up about 6:30.

"Great! Then you can see my new security measures."

That confused me. "Nick's still out of town. I know you haven't had the camera installed yet."

"No, that'll be later in the week, but I have to do something in the meantime to protect myself from the serial killer."

I just hoped her security measures didn't involve firearms.

It was still early afternoon. So, after finding her address in the directory, I walked the two blocks to Miranda Overstreet's house. I'd learned over the years that people are more likely to talk face to face than they are on the phone.

EIGHTEEN

MIRANDA OVERSTREET LIVED ON LEAFY TRACE IN THE MEAD-
ows. She answered the door dressed for tennis.

"Hi, Miranda. I'm Emily." I purposely didn't use my last name.
"I live over in The Village. And I'm trying to learn a little more
about Sarah Christopher. The family still has a lot of questions."

She gave me a quizzical look. "They asked *you* ...?"

"I'm a retired police officer. They thought I could look into it
for them." I hoped that was enough of an explanation. I really didn't
want to go through the whole ex-husband thing again. "It won't
take long, but you look like you're on your way out. I can come
back later, if that's better."

"No, come on in. I've got a few minutes," she said with a smile.
"We don't play for another hour and if I get there early, I'll just have
to stand around and wait."

The directory had listed her with her husband, Jerry, but the
house was quiet and I guessed he was out. We talked in the living
room where two big double windows let in a flood of natural light.

"What happened to Sarah is just so sad. I can't believe her husband killed her. And Becky, too!"

"Yeah, it's a terrible situation," I agreed, "but his children aren't convinced Owen did it. It does look bad, but they want to see a little more investigation done."

She nodded, eyes wide. "What do you want to ask me?"

"I understand that you and Sarah were friends?"

"Yeah, we were. I wouldn't say we were that close, but we played bridge together and we occasionally went to the mall or out to lunch."

"How often did you go up to Cherokee with her?" I asked matter-of-factly.

Several emotions played across her face. She decided to deny it. "You mean North Carolina? I never went there with Sarah."

"Come on, Miranda. I know you went at least once." She wasn't the only one who could lie.

She let a long minute pass before finally saying, "Okay. I did. I went three times." Her desperate eyes held mine. "But Jerry doesn't know. And I don't want him to! He'd think I was crazy if he found out I went to a casino and gambled!"

"I don't have any reason to tell him."

She looked relieved at that.

"Did Becky go with you?"

She nodded. "Usually, but Sarah always drove. She knew where to go and just how to get there. It's a big place, but she knew her way around."

"Anybody else?"

"Well, Carolyn Grundy went every time I did. And there were two or three other women that came sometimes, too. But I didn't know them. They were in another car. One was named Ann, I think. And there was Ilsa or Elsa, never knew which. Oh, and one more." She shook her head. "I don't know what her real name was.

Everybody called her Cricket. She's this tiny little thing, real petite, with red hair."

I made note of the names while Miranda fidgeted in her chair, moving from one position to another.

"Emily," she blurted out, "I only went three times.! And I didn't do anything terrible. We just had fun. But we'd be gone all day and Jerry started asking a lot of questions. I knew he'd be furious if he found out I was wasting money like that. He always says gambling is stupid. So I stopped going."

"He won't hear about any of this from me," I reassured her.

I asked a few more questions, but didn't get anything else useful. Then Miranda went off to her tennis match and I walked home.

It was still light that evening when I pulled into Linda's drive — the one thing about the early start to Daylight Savings Time that I liked. Angel started barking as soon as I walked to the door. I rang the bell.

"Just a sec," I heard Linda call out, but several minutes passed, accompanied by some strange scraping noises, before she opened the door.

At least, she partially opened the door. Its progress was halted by a dining room chair in the foyer and I had to squeeze in sideways.

She gave me a quick hug. "I know that chair won't keep out anybody who really wants to get in, but I'll sure hear them if they try."

She took me on a quick tour.

"See," she said, showing me the little screw-on metal pieces she'd put into the tracks of the upper window frames. "I bought them for all the windows. Now nobody can raise one more than five inches."

I had to admit that was a good idea and thought I might try it at my house, but I wasn't as eager to embrace the other measures she'd taken.

More chairs were positioned in front of the other exterior doors and she'd used twine to tie metal spatulas and spoons to the handle of her bedroom door.

"That way, if someone tries to open it, it'll make noise. And when I go to bed, I'm going to put a lot of pots and pans on the floor in the hallway. Anyone trying to sneak in when it's dark won't see them and they'll trip."

She sneezed.

"Are you still having allergy problems?" I asked.

"Yeah. The medicine I bought hasn't really helped. Guess I'm going to have to see a doctor."

The security tour continued in her bedroom, where she had two canisters of pepper spray on the bedside table and a baseball bat leaning against a wall.

"There's pepper spray in the bathroom, too."

I felt awful that I hadn't really appreciated how frightened she was.

"I honestly don't think you have anything to worry about, but you're certainly prepared."

She nodded enthusiastically. "Yes, I know. No one is getting in tonight. And after tomorrow, it'll be okay. I called an alarm company. They'll be here in the morning to install equipment on the doors and windows."

Angel had been following us from room to room, hoping for some attention. I leaned down and patted her head.

"The alarm is a great idea. I know that will make you feel better. But Angel's barking is probably the best deterrent there is. She sounded fierce when I got here today. Nobody wants to break into a house with a dog."

"Oh, she's too sweet to scare anybody. She thinks people were put on this earth just to pet her and play with her."

After Linda made sure Angel's water bowl was full and all the doors were securely locked, we drove to The Good Grain. We had our choice of tables and selected a booth on the right side where we could look out onto the street.

"I just wish we could figure out who my stalker is," she said after we ordered. "I haven't had a decent night's sleep in a week!"

"Maybe you will once your alarm system is installed." I changed the subject, hoping to distract her from her fears. "So, have you heard anything more about the suspicious parties?"

She shook her head. "All anybody's been talking about lately are the killings. But last week I did hear that someone spotted a couple of good-looking young men going into a house up in The Meadows, carrying boxes. And there was a party there that night. Do you think they might have been, you know, paid escorts?"

"It's more likely they were delivery men or maybe caterers."

She shrugged, already disinterested in the subject. Neighborhood orgies had lost their conversational appeal since there'd been two murders in a week.

After we'd started on our vegetarian, non-dairy pizza, I told Linda what I'd learned and what I thought Sarah had been up to.

"I'm pretty sure that she was gambling."

"Gambling? Like lottery tickets? Or bingo?"

"No. I think she and Becky Cartwright were going up to Cherokee to gamble in the casinos there. They might have gone to Alabama, too."

Her mouth dropped open. "There are casinos in *Alabama*?"

"Yeah. Several of them, mostly around Montgomery, I think. But Cherokee's closer."

She spent a minute or two in thought as we both enjoyed the food. Then her eyes lit up. "The money she spent and the way she was trying to improve her luck! If she was hooked on gambling, it all makes perfect sense."

I nodded. "But I don't see how it could have caused their deaths. So I'm still at square one."

I took another bite, still thinking about what I'd learned. "A strange thing though. After all the time she'd spent there since last fall, it doesn't look like Sarah went to Cherokee at all last month. Or if she did, she wasn't driving her own car up there."

"But she was still going through their money at an amazing rate. Either she was gambling somewhere else or one of her friends was driving them to the casinos. Sarah didn't make any gas or motel charges in March."

I took a minute to eat more pizza, then said, "And none of that—the gambling, the trips to Cherokee, the money she was withdrawing—none of that gets me any closer to finding a reason for the killings. The only way it makes sense is if Owen did kill them. And I just can't accept that."

For the rest of the meal, we kept the conversation as light as we could. Grandchildren and Linda's shop. She was having a good year, in both sales and class enrollment.

"I can hardly keep up. It's like people are suddenly experiencing a spiritual rebirth."

I smiled. "Well, it couldn't come at a better time."

I expected a relaxing evening at home, but Curtis changed all that. He spent the time I was away expressing his displeasure with my absence. He'd shoved the morning paper off the coffee table and shredded it. It must have been a frenzied attack. Torn newsprint was scattered all around the room and ragged little pieces of paper were everywhere, on and under the furniture and all over the floor.

I'd have scolded him, but knew that never did any good. As I gathered and swept up the mess, I wondered if I was going to have to bring a second cat into the house. Maybe if he had company, he wouldn't get so stressed when I left him.

Once that was done, I gave some thought to Nick's homecoming the next day. We'd discussed going out, but having a nice dinner at home could be more pleasant. I checked the freezer and found a small pork loin. It should thaw nicely in the fridge and be perfect for tomorrow night.

NINETEEN

I WOKE UP WITH A CERTAINTY THAT I NEEDED TO GO TO Cherokee that day. I knew I was grasping at straws, but Sarah and Becky had spent considerable time there. Since no other avenue of investigation had produced anything helpful, I felt like I had to at least see the place.

There was an alarm company van parked in Linda's driveway when I left the house. I hoped having a security system put in would ease her fears.

The last time I'd traveled to the mountains, the weather had been perfect and I'd been on the back of Nick's motorcycle. Wednesday was different. I was alone in my CR-V and the weather was nasty. While I was spared the storms of the last week, the day was overcast with intermittent rain showers, some light, some heavy.

Nick and I had taken a scenic route, but my GPS kept me on main highways during the two-hour drive to Cherokee. I kept the music low. The rain, wet roads, and moderate traffic demanded my full attention.

The casino in North Carolina was something of a surprise. Knowing that it was run by the Cherokees, I guess I'd expected something tribal or at least more atmospherically native American.

Instead I found a huge modern casino complex spread out around a sleek, twenty-something-story hotel. It looked like it had been picked up in Las Vegas and deposited among the picturesque peaks of the Blue Ridge Mountains.

Parking near the casino wasn't difficult, even though there were already quite a few cars in the lot, more than I would have expected to see at 11:30 on a Wednesday morning. Inside was a huge open space that looked a lot like other casinos I'd visited over the years. There were banks of slot machines lining the walls and quite a few of them were in use, players pushing buttons and watching screens with grim concentration. Tables for poker, black jack, and other games were scattered throughout, but only a few of those were in operation. Evidently the early crowd preferred the slots.

Casino employees moved unobtrusively around the floor. Cashiers sat in cages to one side and watched the show in front of them. As I wandered through, I passed a couple of restaurants in the process of setting up for lunch service.

An excited female shout came from the slots area. Seemed like someone was a winner. I looked over in time to see the machine spit out the ticket that she would take to the cashiers for payment of her win. While I knew money was money, I kind of missed the old slots where coins gushed from the machine when someone hit a jackpot.

I spoke to several of the employees, showing them Sarah's picture, but never found anyone who admitted to seeing her. The result was the same with the cashiers behind their protective metal mesh. I wasn't surprised. Hundreds of people came through here every day. It had been a long shot to hope someone would remember a woman who visited a few times back in the winter.

As I expected, the casino was a strictly cash operation. Players either brought money with them or got it from the numerous ATMs in the place. With the exception of the restaurants, credit cards were useless here.

After half an hour or so, I was beginning to feel a little embarrassed that I'd driven up here on a whim with no clear plan of action. I hadn't learned anything new. Hell, I hadn't learned anything at all.

To emphasize the futility of my trip, I discovered that this wasn't the only casino in the area. There were several more within fifty miles or so. Sarah could have gambled in any of them. After striking out here, there was no reason to believe my luck would be different in the other locations.

My impulsive behavior had brought me all the way up here on a fool's errand. I was about to leave, having accomplished exactly nothing, when I saw something on the far side of the casino that stopped me.

Two men and a woman, all dressed in what I now recognized as casino uniforms, were working around the empty gaming tables, readying them for later in the day. There was nothing remarkable about the woman or one of the men, but the second man looked familiar. Tall with a long blond ponytail, he resembled the man I'd seen talking with an officer at the accident scene in Marchpoint Saturday evening.

I started across the casino floor, but the three turned and moved quickly in the opposite direction. Before I could reach them, they had disappeared through a double door on the far wall. When I got there a minute later, I saw that the doors were marked Employees Only.

My first impulse was to push on through and find the guy

with the ponytail, but I realized it wasn't a smart idea. First of all, I couldn't swear he was the same man. Tall guys with long ponytails weren't exactly rare. I knew several attorneys who sported the look.

But even if he were the same man, all he'd done was drive into Marchpoint and get hit by one of my stop-sign-running neighbors. There were lots of reasons he might have been there, none of which had to be associated with Sarah's and Becky's deaths. Before confronting a complete stranger, I needed a lot more information.

I returned to my car in a steady drizzle, knowing I'd wasted a lot of time. But the day wasn't a total loss. It was just after noon and there was plenty of time to get home and make that special dinner for Nick.

The thought of driving miles of wet, crowded highways was definitely not appealing. I changed the settings on the GPS to direct me home using backroads, hit the Select Route button and let the mechanical voice lead me.

It was a wet, gray day and the wipers swept monotonously back and forth to clear the windshield. But in spite of the rain, I was enjoying the drive. The roads twisted and turned around and through the mountains. There were times when I was the only car in sight.

I had plenty of time to think. The man with the ponytail was a puzzle. A crazy idea occurred to me. Maybe he ran a shuttle for gamblers between Marchpoint and Cherokee, but I discarded the thought almost as quickly as it came. That just didn't make sense. The casinos certainly weren't hurting for business and the few people that a shuttle could deliver there wouldn't make much difference, not to mention the cost of operation and the liability that went along with transporting passengers.

I steered into an especially sharp curve and slowed the car at about the same time a big truck appeared from the opposite direction. It veered into my lane and there was a sudden blast of a horn. Then it was gone, but the damage was done.

I'd swerved to miss the truck and ended up on the narrow shoulder where I had a sickening glimpse of the sharp drop off to the right. Jerking the wheel to the left to get back onto the pavement, I overcorrected. I braked and the back of the SUV fishtailed. Steering into it, I took my foot off the brake pedal until the car slowed on its own and I came to a stop, facing the direction from which I'd come.

I exhaled — realizing that I'd been holding my breath — then slowly drove to a service station I'd passed a few miles back. Once I parked in the lot, I sent up a prayer of thanks. I hadn't been hurt and the vehicle was undamaged. The only casualty was my purse that had flown off the passenger seat and dumped its contents on the floor.

Ignoring the rain, which was now falling more heavily, I got out, went around to the passenger side, and opened the door. I grabbed everything I could lay my hands on — wallet, phone, checkbook, lipstick — and jammed it back into the bag. While I was reaching under the seat for things I might have missed, my hand brushed an unfamiliar object. I pulled it out and saw the fairy cross I'd been carrying around for days.

I am not superstitious, but it gave me pause. This little stone was supposed to bring good luck. Another foot or two to the right and my car would have been rolling down the side of a mountain. I'd certainly been lucky, and not just today. The stone had also been with me when I avoided being struck by a car at the stop sign, and when the tornado narrowly missed my house. No, I wasn't superstitious, but I knew I'd be carrying the fairy cross with me from then on.

TWENTY

NICK WAS DRESSED FOR A RESTAURANT DINNER IN DARK pants and a navy sports coat when he rang my doorbell at 5:30. I, on the other hand, was wearing worn jeans and a T shirt. After a quick kiss, he held me by the shoulders and gave my outfit an up-and-down look.

"I thought we were going up to the lake for dinner." Then he sniffed the air. "But it seems I was mistaken."

"Well, it's your first night back and I wanted you all to myself."

He grinned. "I like the sound of that."

"Good. I have a pitcher of martinis waiting and a pork loin stuffed with apples in the oven. Oh, and the Braves game will be on in a little while."

He gave me a hug. "That's better than the lake could ever be." He took off his coat, hung it on the rack in the hall, and rolled up his shirt sleeves.

Over martinis, we caught up on the last few days. He told me about his work in Alabama and I shared my experiences.

"Andrew's so concerned about Owen's arrest," I told him. "He's flying in tomorrow afternoon. I'm picking him up at the airport, but he'll be staying with his father."

"Of course, he wants to be here," Nick said. "What about Chelsea?"

I shook my head. "She's upset, just like she has been since his first arrest, but I think I've convinced her that it's better to stay home with her family for now. There's really nothing she can do here. Of course, if it goes to trial …"

"Let's not worry about that right now."

After dinner, which was good enough that we both had second helpings of the pork, we cuddled up on the sofa to watch the game. Curtis was there, too, edging in between us. It was a lovely evening.

Until it wasn't.

The game ended with a loss just after ten. Nick had already given a couple of exaggerated yawns, but the smile in his eyes made it clear sleep wasn't his main concern. I was about to suggest retiring for the night when frantic pounding on the front door made me jump nearly out of my skin. The pounding was accompanied by repeated ringing of the bell.

I got up. "What in the world —"

Nick stepped quickly past me to reach the door first and flick on the porch light. Through the glass, we saw Linda, still pushing the bell and looking fearfully back over her shoulder.

When Nick opened the door, she nearly knocked him over getting inside.

"Shut the door!" She gasped for breath. "Shut the door! He may still be out there."

Nick and I both looked out toward the street, but didn't see anyone.

Linda was shaking. Her hair was snarled around her head and shoulders, with pieces of leaves and twigs stuck in the tangle. Her blouse and skirt were both torn in several places and she had a shallow scratch across her left cheek.

"Linda, it's okay." I put an arm around her. "You're safe! We'll call the police."

"No!" She stepped away from me. "No police."

"Okay," I said, confused but not wanting to upset her further, "no police."

Nick gently guided her to the sofa where she perched uneasily on the edge of the cushion, still giving the door frequent glances.

"There's no one there," I tried to reassure her. "The door's locked. No one can get in the house and, if they did, they'd have to deal with Nick and me before they ever got to you."

Nick brought her a glass of water and she gulped down half of it. I sat next to her, taking one of her hands in mine, while Nick eased into a chair opposite.

"Now tell us what happened," I said, keeping my voice even and low.

She drank more water and then, still breathing hard and fast, said, "I found out where … where Sarah was … gambling." She stopped for a deep breath. "It was in Marchpoint!"

She needed a minute to calm down. We all sat quietly while she got her thoughts in order. Then she was able to tell her story.

"After dinner yesterday, I got to thinking about what you said," she told me. "You know, how Sarah was gambling in Cherokee and all. But then she quit going up there. Right?"

"Well, I'm not sure that's what happened. I know *she* stopped driving up there. But she could have gone with someone else."

"I don't think so. In fact, I know she didn't. She found a place for her and her friends to gamble *right here*," Linda said. "You've heard of private games, haven't you?"

"Yeah, but never in an active adult neighborhood. Mahjong is more the style here."

She shook her head. "But why wouldn't people here like real gambling? They already award prizes in bingo and trivia, don't they? That's the same thing."

She lifted the glass again, but put it back on the coffee table when she saw it was empty. Nick hurried to the kitchen, refilled it and gave it to her. After four or five swallows, she went on. "The more I thought about it, the more it totally made sense! Actually it made a whole lot more sense than orgies."

"Orgies?" Nick asked.

"See," Linda said, "the rumors were all wrong. Those parties everyone was talking about, they weren't sex parties at all. They're gambling parties."

I nodded.

"You found a gambling party?" Nick asked.

"I did!" she said proudly. "I waited until after dark tonight, nine o'clock maybe. Then I got in my car and just started looking."

"But how did you know there'd be a party tonight?"he asked.

"I didn't, of course. But I was determined to find out if I was right. If I couldn't find a party tonight, I was going to go out looking tomorrow and through the weekend, if I had to. I was just sure I was right."

"So you just drove around?" I asked.

She nodded. "Yeah. You know, this is one big place. I started here in The Village, but there weren't any houses with a bunch of cars parked outside. So next I went through The Meadows. It was

on Cold Spring Court—that's where I found the house with a party going on, down in the cul-de-sac."

"It could have been a big dinner or even a Tupperware party," I
interrupted.

She held up a hand. "Just wait. You're right. It could have been
anything. I knew I had to get a look in the house to be sure. But I
couldn't think of any reason to go up and knock on the door. So ... I
turned around and parked up on Evergreen Circle, then sneaked
through the backyards until I got to the house where the party was
going on. First I tried to look in the side windows."

Nick was staring at her as if he'd never seen her before. And
I was having a hard time picturing Linda, in sandals and a long,
flouncy skirt, creeping through backyards in the dark.

"But the curtains were closed. There wasn't even a tiny gap
I could see through." She sounded annoyed. "If there had been,
everything would have been okay. But I had to go to the back and
look through the sliding glass doors.

"I was real quiet when I got to the patio, really took my time,
and then I could see everything! It was like something in the movies.
There was a poker game going on in the dining room and another
one in the kitchen. They'd pushed all the living room furniture back
against the walls and set up one of those long tables where people
were throwing dice. What's it called?"

"Craps," Nick supplied.

"Yes, that's it. Everybody was drinking and laughing and playing games. There must have been twenty people there!"

I nodded, impressed at what she'd discovered. "It sounds like
you found the Marchpoint gambling den."

She gave a small smile. "Yeah, but then things went bad real fast.

I was standing all the way to one side of the glass door, just looking around the edge of the frame, you know? I thought I was out of sight, but someone looked up and saw me peeking in. All of a sudden there was a bunch of yelling and then one guy came running to the back door!"

She closed her eyes, reliving her fright. Then took a deep, steadying breath.

"What did you do?" Nick asked.

Her eyes snapped open. "I took off, of course! I ran like crazy. I was already a couple of doors down when I heard him come out of the house. I just looked back once and saw this big guy chasing me. I was running back the way I came, but when I got up to Evergreen, he was too close for me to get to the car. I knew he'd catch me if I went that way, out in the open."

She swallowed hard, as if pushing down the memory of her fear. "So I went the other way, into the woods behind the houses on Evergreen.

"Was he still chasing you?" I asked.

"I couldn't tell. It was dark and couldn't see much for the woods around me. But I didn't want to go back towards the car. I could have run right into him! So I worked my way down the hill to the walking trail, the one that comes out on Alcovy Drive. After that I just came here."

"That's several miles away," Nick said. "You must be exhausted."

"I think I am," she said, relaxing enough to sit back against the cushion. "The worst part was walking along the streets. Every time I heard a car coming, I had to hide behind a bush or a tree. I was scared to death he'd find me."

"Linda, why didn't you call me?"

"Phone's locked in the car, with my purse."

"Well, I still think we ought to call the police," I said.

But she shook her head. "No! I know gambling is illegal, but so is going onto someone's property to look in their windows. Those people could press charges. I might get arrested!"

I sighed. "All right."

"We ought to go back for your car right now," Nick said. "Do you have the keys?"

She put a hand over her skirt pocket. "Yeah, they're still here."

TWENTY-ONE

WE TOOK NICK'S CAR FOR THE QUICK DRIVE TO EVERGREEN Circle. Linda's eight-year-old Volvo was right where she said it would be, but Nick didn't stop there. Instead he turned onto Cold Spring Court. The cul-de-sac was alive with people, all dressed for an evening out. They were climbing into cars, laughing and talking loudly in the quiet night. Two vehicles passed us driving away from the house. I recognized one of the drivers as Miranda Overstreet.

"Looks like you broke up the party," Nick said.

"They must not have been all that concerned about me." Linda glanced at her watch. "I left here over an hour ago."

"Well, they're breaking it up now," I said. "It's just after 11:00. I'd guess most of these parties go on considerably later."

A Jeep pulled away from the curb, followed a few seconds later by a Toyota.

"I'll say!" Linda said, then she qualified that. "At least, that's what I've heard."

Nick did a quick turn around and started back up the street.

"Aren't we going to confront them?" Linda asked.

"We're not cops. Don't see what it would accomplish," I told her. "We already know what was going on. I'm assuming Sarah was came to the games, but I'd like confirmation. I can come back to-morrow and see if they'll talk to me."

We dropped Linda at her car and waited until she was inside and started it. She drove off and Nick followed.

He cleared his throat, a sure sign he had something to say that he wasn't comfortable with. "Even if Sarah was going to these games, I don't know that it's going to make any difference. You already knew she was gambling. Does it matter where she did it?"

"No, I guess not."

He reached for my hand. "Emily, you've made it clear you feel obligated to help, but everything you've found so far just makes Owen look more guilty."

"I've noticed that myself."

He released my hand and turned the car onto our street. "Then what are you doing?"

"I know it seems like I'm beating my head against a wall. But if there's a chance ... for the kids, I have to keep looking."

He drove into his driveway, turned off the car and pulled me close. "And I'll stand by you, whatever you need to do." He kissed me. "I love you."

"And I love you, too." I opened the car door. "Now let's get back to my place. As I recall, before we were interrupted, you were saying how tired you were."

We walked across the cul-de-sac and Nick gave a couple more theatrical yawns. Then he smiled broadly. "You're right. I think we should go right to bed."

As eager as I was to talk to Miranda and find out about last night's gambling party, there was no time for that Thursday morning. Drew's flight was due at 12:50. A veteran of Atlanta's legendary traffic, I knew enough to leave my house by 11:15. Even so, I cut it close. We'd arranged to meet outside the terminal to save me the trouble of parking. I only drove the complete multi-lane circuit past the terminal and back around twice. The third time I spotted him at the curb in front of the Delta entrance. A green Chrysler entered the traffic lane as I approached and I quickly pulled into the spot he'd vacated.

Andrew jogged down to where I was. He threw his bag in the back seat and got in beside me. We exchanged a quick hug, then I pulled away from the sidewalk and rejoined the parade of departing cars. Picking someone up at Hartsfield-Jackson Airport is like taking part in a relay race. You're always changing positions with the other drivers and every move must be executed in the shortest possible time.

"This place is busier every time I come home!"

"Yep. You might have heard—Atlanta has the busiest airport in the world."

He laughed. "And that's something to be proud of?"

"No. It's just a fact of life around here." I smiled at him. "It's so good to see you, Drew."

Seattle hadn't changed him. He was as handsome as ever—trim, tall, with thick brown hair, and a neatly-trimmed goatee. He'd inherited his father's good looks. But today those looks were marred by dark circles under his eyes and a distracted expression.

"It's good to see you, too, Mom."

"How was your flight?"

"Okay," he said, impatient with small talk. "What's going on with Dad? Has anything else happened?"

"He's doing all right, I guess. But I imagine he's getting a little stir crazy since he can't leave the house. The ankle monitor, you know." I stopped talking as I maneuvered back onto the expressway. Once we'd joined the river of cars and I'd worked my way over into a middle lane, I could continue. "Having you there will make him a lot happier."

"I hope so. Dad said that you're looking into the murders for him. Have you found anything to prove he didn't do this?" he asked.

"No, but there was some strange stuff going on."

It took a good fifteen minutes to tell him about the two deaths and Sarah's gambling. I finished with Linda finding the party the night before.

"You're kidding! Whoever heard of a gambling den in a *retirement* community?"

"Active adult," I corrected automatically.

He laughed. "What? Do they play in the afternoon? I thought people of a certain age liked to get to bed early."

I poked him in the ribs. "We're not all ancient and infirm. Some of us have even stayed awake past midnight on occasion. And I've heard these parties go until all hours."

Then I sobered. "But nothing I've discovered has cleared your dad. If anything, it's just given him a stronger motive. She was spending their money at an insane rate."

He absorbed that in silence for a few minutes, then asked, "But why would he kill that other woman?"

I shrugged. "The police seem to think Becky was there when he killed Sarah and that he went after her to keep her from talking."

"Well, they're wrong! I'll never believe my father could kill anyone!"

I had no way to comfort him and we drove for a bit in silence. It wasn't until we'd passed through the city that Drew spoke again.

"So tell me more about Nick. I'm looking forward to meeting him. You've sounded pretty happy when we've talked about him."

I nodded, smiling. "He's a special man. I think you'll like him."

"Maybe when all this is over …"

"Yeah. You can meet him then."

I dropped Drew at Owen's place, but didn't go in with him. Their reunion was going to be difficult enough without me there. Instead, I drove again to Miranda Overstreet's house, pulling my car into the drive behind hers. I rang the bell and knocked several times before the door finally opened.

To be blunt, Miranda looked like hell. Her hair was limp and needed a good washing. Her eyes were red and her shoulders drooped as if a huge weight was bearing down on her. She didn't look like the same woman I'd last seen on her way to play tennis.

"I knew someone would come," she said, stepping back to let me in the house. "I guess that was you looking in the window at Carol's last night."

"Not me, but someone I know. I thought you only went with Sarah three times."

She looked at me with sad eyes. "I did. But this is different. This is just some people getting together in the neighborhood. You're not going to tell Jerry, are you? After all, we were just having a little fun! We weren't hurting anyone."

"Gambling is still illegal in Georgia, Miranda."

She tried for outrage. "Really? Well, somebody better tell the government because I'm pretty sure playing the state lottery is gambling."

"I agree with you, but that doesn't change the law."

She sighed and dropped into a chair at the kitchen table. I sat across from her. There were three daffodils in a glass vase on the table top, a cheerful little touch of spring.

"Look, I don't care what you do for fun," I told her. "And I still don't have any reason to tell your husband. But what's going on here isn't just a friendly poker game among friends. It's organized gambling. Someone has to run the operation, bring in the equipment, set up the bank, all that stuff. And I'm pretty sure it's not your friend Carol."

She was nodding as I spoke.

"So who is it?"

"I don't know." She saw my doubt. "No, really, I don't have any idea."

"Then how do you know when the games are held? And where? They can't all be at Carol's house."

"No. Always different places, different days."

"Then how do you know where to go?" I asked impatiently.

"Email."

"*Email*?"

"Yeah. I know it sounds crazy, but that's how we do it."

I shook my head. "So who sends the emails?"

She shrugged. "Nobody knows. They just started showing up. From someone called Lucky Lady. They tell us where to go and when. That's all."

"So who decides where the parties are going to be held?"

"Lucky Lady asks for volunteers to host a party. If you agree to have it at your house, she takes care of sending out the invitations. And getting the equipment delivered and the guys to run the show. And...you get a $300 bonus to be the hostess! That's easy money right there. Of course, I never could do it because of Jerry."

I was amazed at the simplicity of the operation. "Do you still have any of the emails on your computer?"

"Oh, no, I delete them as soon as I put the date on my calendar. I couldn't let Jerry find them!"

"So some of them should still be in your trash file, right?"

"I guess so," she said worriedly. "I never thought about that."

At my urging, she brought out her laptop and a few minutes later, we were looking at several messages sent from Lady Luck at gmail. The address was a disappointment. Anyone can get a gmail account under any name. It would take a subpoena to find out any more and, even then, the most we could hope for was an IP address for Lady Luck's computer. If the sender really wanted to hide his identity, he wouldn't send the messages from his home computer. There were plenty if public computers he could use in libraries or cafes.

I didn't know what I might need them for, but I had Miranda print out the messages for me.

Before I left, she asked me one more time not to tell Jerry about her gambling.

"I won't, but you may want to tell him yourself. This is a murder investigation, after all. You never can tell what will come out in the end. And I want you to call me the next time you get an email from Lucky Lady."

The back door opened and a short, wiry, gray-haired man came into the kitchen.

He smiled and crossed over to Miranda to give her a kiss on the cheek. "Hey, babe, didn't know you were expecting company."

Miranda sat frozen in her chair. I've never seen color leave a person's face as fast as it drained from hers. I thought she was going to pass out.

I jumped up. "Hey. I'm Emily Christopher," I said, extending my hand to the man I assumed was Jerry. Miranda's face was twisted in an expression of terror.

"I'm Jerry Overstreet. Nice to meet you."

"I just stopped by to try and talk Miranda into helping us," I improvised. "We have an opening on the Marchpoint Entertainment Committee and we think she'd do a fantastic job! She's agreed to consider it."

I figured I might as well make it as easy for her as I could. Nothing would be gained by creating problems for her and Jerry, and she might be grateful enough to call me when she heard from Lucky Lady again.

Miranda almost glowed with relief. "Uh … that's right. It sounds like it would be fun, but I told her I'd have to think about it."

"Well, good, good. You might enjoy it." Jerry was already opening the fridge. "Can I offer you some iced tea?"

"Oh, no. I've got to run. But it was nice to meet you. Call me when you know something, Miranda."

TWENTY-TWO

BACK IN THE CAR, I CHECKED MY PHONE—NO CALLS, NO messages. That was a relief. I hoped it meant Owen and Drew were getting along okay. They'd always had a loving, but prickly relationship.

Curtis was waiting at the back door when I got home. Evidently I'd been gone a long while in cat time. He cried as I came in, winding around my feet when I walked across the kitchen. But once I reached down and rubbed his head, he left me for his food bowl where he started crunching the kibble.

A quick check of the neighborhood directory revealed that Carol and Edward Johansen lived at 2112 Cold Spring Court, the site of last night's party. Even though results are usually better when you talk to people in person, I wasn't sure this was one of those times. After last night, I doubted I'd get a very warm reception from the party hosts. So I dialed the number and, after two rings, it was answered by a deep-voiced man.

"I wanted to talk to you about the party you had last night," I began.

"So *you're* the one who was snooping around my house!" he said angrily.

"No, that was someone else. I came later, when everyone was leaving."

"Well, let me tell you one damn thing, lady. This is my house and I'll do whatever I please here. Now leave me the hell alone."

With that the connection was broken. I knew better than to call back. Then I realized I didn't really need to. If they were like Miranda, they wouldn't have any information about the organizer either.

It seemed likely that the person who set up the gambling parties was one of the women who had gone to Cherokee with Sarah and Becky. Otherwise, how would Lucky Lady know who to email? That's where I needed to concentrate my efforts. Since Sarah and Becky were both dead, they could be eliminated and it was unlikely to be Miranda. It had to be one of the others.

I sat down at the table with a pen and a legal pad and wrote the names that Miranda had given me. Carolyn Grundy, Ann, Ilse (or Elsa) and Cricket. Then I went back to the directory.

I found Carolyn Grundy with no trouble. She lived in The Village, only a block away from me. I made note of her address, then paged through the directory. There were over ten women named Ann or Anne, plus two Mary Annes, and several other variations. I wasn't going to find the right one that way.

Ilsa was another story. There was an Ilsa McGinnis and an Elsa Chambers. Looking at their pictures (yes, our directory has pictures of all our residents), I decided Ilsa McGinnis was the most likely candidate. She was a fit single woman who looked to be in her late 50s, about the same age as the other Cherokee gamblers. Elsa Chambers, on the other hand, was married and, judging by the picture, probably fifteen or twenty years older. I couldn't see her arranging anything like a gambling ring. But you never knew, so I'd try talking to both of them.

There was no Cricket listed and I wasn't surprised. Nicknames weren't used in the directory, but there was a good chance I could find her by asking around at the clubhouse. My to-do list just kept growing. The sad part was that I didn't know whether I was doing any good at all.

UPS delivered a package to my door late that afternoon. Given the size of the box, it was lighter than I expected when I picked it up. I found out why when I opened it.

Inside, layered in sheets of white tissue paper, was a dress. And not just any dress. It was a gauzy, off the shoulder, peach-colored dress.

"Oh, my goodness."

The enclosed note was unnecessary. It couldn't have been from anyone but Ariel. In a flowing hand, she'd written:

When I saw this dress, I knew it was perfect for you. Please accept it with my love. I guessed at the size, but it should be close.

You'll be beautiful. See you at the wedding!

Ariel

Annette's mother was a woman accustomed to getting her way, I knew, but not this time. I couldn't accept the dress. I'd just have to find a tactful way to return it. In the meantime, I knew better than to leave it within Curtis's curious reach. So I arranged it carefully on a wooden hanger and found a spot in my closet where no other clothes were touching it.I ate alone Thursday night, unless you counted Curtis, who sat at my feet and stared at me through the entire meal. I'd never given him a scrap from the table, but he was always hopeful. Nick was at a dinner meeting in Atlanta. He'd said he'd come by when he got home if it wasn't too late.

I reached for the phone after dinner. Carolyn Grundy wasn't happy to hear from me, but she didn't sound surprised. I thought it was likely that Miranda had warned her I might call. At least she was nicer than Edward Johansen had been. She wasn't happy about it, but she answered my few questions. Like Becky and Sarah, she'd been a regular visitor to the casinos in Cherokee.

"Who else went with you?"

"Someone named Miranda. A couple of others, but I don't think I ever heard their names. I mean, we didn't chat. We were going up there to gamble."

"So how did you find out about the gambling parties here in Marchpoint?"

Her story was the same as Miranda's—she'd gotten her invitations by email and never knew who sent them. But there was one difference.

"One day I got a message from Lucky Lady asking if I'd like to host a party. She said she'd take care of everything, just like always. All I had to provide were drinks and snacks for the party. And she'd pay me $300. So I did it!"

"You hosted one of the parties? How did that go?"

"Oh, it was great," she said. "Her people came and set everything up. The nice young men ran all the games and after it was over, they packed up and left. And one of them handed me $300—in cash! It was the easiest money I ever made."

"Did one of those nice young men have a long ponytail?"

"Why, yes. How did you know?"

"Lucky guess. So who is Lucky Lady?"

There was a brief pause, then she said, "I don't have any idea. I never met her."

"Are you sure? You must have talked to her when you were scheduling the party."

"No. Nothing but the emails."

I didn't believe her, but I didn't have any leverage to persuade her to tell me the truth. "Are you sure? I really need to find her."

"I'm sure."

"Okay. Well, Maybe the police can trace the emails." I threw that out, but, even as I said it, I thought it was probably an empty threat.

By then, it was almost nine and I didn't like calling strangers this late. I'd leave the others until the next day. Instead I dialed the number of someone I knew would be awake. Drew answered on the second ring.

"Everything's fine here," he told me. "We ordered in and now Dad's in the office working. Even though he can't leave, he can still work from home. His paralegal brought some files to him today."

I wondered if the paralegal was Jane Carelli and if Drew had met his next stepmother.

"Are you two getting along okay?" I asked.

Over the years Drew and Owen had had some serious conflicts. Owen expected his son to follow him into the legal profession, but the law held no interest for Drew. He'd always been technologically minded and followed his passion. When he moved to Seattle three years ago, that had just made matters between them worse. Owen always felt that his son's moving to the other side of the country was a slap in his face.

"Actually, we are," Drew said with some surprise in his voice.

"He really seems to appreciate that I came to be with him. We've had some serious conversations already. I think this trip is going to be good for both of us."

It was nice to get some good news for a change.

As the evening passed, images of the peach dress kept intruding into my thoughts. Finally I gave up trying to resist. I went into the bedroom, undressed, gently pulled the dress from its hanger, and slipped it over my head. The fabric was a light whisper settling on my skin.

I turned to look at myself in the mirror and almost gasped in surprise. I'd never looked so glamorous. Ariel had been spot-on as far as size went. Actually, she was spot-on with everything! It was a dress that would have been right at home on any red carpet in the world.

The doorbell interrupted my self-admiration. It was Nick and, as he came in, an expression of wonder washed over his face.

"Emily, you're gorgeous!" He took me in his arms, kissed me, then ran his lips over my bare shoulders. "You're like something out of a dream!"

We progressed quickly from the foyer to the bedroom, stopping every few feet for another embrace. As I slipped carefully out of the magical dress, I knew there was no way I'd ever return it.

TWENTY-THREE

WE WERE UP EARLY FRIDAY MORNING. THE DOORBELL CAM-
eras he'd ordered had arrived and Nick was anxious to get them
installed.

"I promised Linda I'd get it done," he said. "And I got the impression it's important to her."

"You have no idea. She did have an alarm system installed and
I think that's helped her feel a lot more secure. But she's still frantic
to find out who's been leaving those cards."

"Let's hope this helps her do just that."

The first thing I did after he left was call Annette.

"You won't believe what I got yesterday."

"You'll have to give me more information than that if you want
me to guess."

"Your mother sent me a dress for the wedding."

"Oh, no! I told her not to. Emily, I'm so sorry."

I laughed. "Don't apologize. It's gorgeous! It's the most wonderful dress I've ever had."

"Really?" She sounded doubtful.

"Yes, really. When I opened the box, my first thought was to return it immediately. Like we'd already talked about, I wasn't interested in a bridesmaid dress. But, Annette, this isn't a bridesmaid dress. When I put it on...I can't tell you how exquisite it is! I just hope it won't be too dressy for your wedding. I know you want it to be casual."

She laughed. "You don't have to worry about that. She got me a dress, too! Listening to you just now was like deja vu. I was going to refuse it until I tried it on. Emily, it makes me feel like a goddess! As soon as Scott saw me in it, he insisted it was perfect for the wedding. He's even going to wear a suit! So, once again, Ariel got her way."

"She did. Are you even surprised?"

Annette laughed. "No. Not at all."

"But I do insist on paying her for the dress," I said.

"Good luck with that. I've already tried and she won't even hear of it. But you can take it up with her yourself."

With the rest of the morning ahead of me, I was determined to finish the cases I had for Annette. That would leave the afternoon to talk with the other gamblers. After that there would be nothing else to do for Owen.

I'd write it all up and give my findings to his attorney. There was nothing earth-shattering in what I'd found and it certainly didn't prove someone else had killed Sarah, but I was sure Mike could weave parts of it through his defense to help establish some reasonable doubt.

Breakfast was a smoothie in front of the computer, followed by two cups of coffee. I was almost done with the work when the doorbell rang.

I'd be lying if I said I wasn't surprised to see Anna Lumpkin standing there with a foil-covered plate in her hands. She was dressed in a tailored navy pantsuit with a ruffled white blouse, more suitable for a board meeting than a neighborly visit. A sleek designer purse hung from one forearm. Her short white hair was perfectly coiffed and her make up looked as if she'd just applied it. As I let her in, she gave me a big smile.

"Chocolate chip cookies," she said, handing me the plate. "They're still warm."

"Wow! That's an unexpected treat. Thank you so much!"

She followed me into the kitchen where I put the plate on the counter.

"Well, I wanted to do something nice for you, dear. After all the time you've put into trying to help Owen."

"Oh, I don't think I've done much."

"That's not what I hear." The neighborhood gossip mill had probably reported my every move. "You've talked to a lot of people. I think it's so admirable that you'd do that for your ex-husband."

I tried to smile, but wasn't very successful. "It was more for the children than for Owen. Would you like a cup of coffee?"

"Oh, no, thanks," she said. "It's nearly twelve. No caffeine after noon is my rule." She gave a little laugh. "Otherwise, I'll never get to sleep tonight."

We settled in the living room and she asked if I'd learned anything that might help Owen.

I shrugged. "Not really. At least nothing that would exonerate him."

"Is it true that *gambling* is going on in our neighborhood?"

I suddenly realized that Anna's real mission might not have been an act of generosity. It was possible she'd come to find out what

I'd discovered so she could contribute to the grapevine. But since she'd already heard about the gambling, I didn't think confirming it would hurt anything. Maybe it would bring her some coveted credibility in the world of Marchpoint gossip.

So I said, "Yes, it is. Guess you just never know what's happening around you."

She pursed her lips together. "Well, I for one am disappointed to hear that. I've always thought of this place as removed, kind of insulated from the worst that the world has to offer."

I nodded. "I guess that's what we all hoped for when we moved here."

Curtis wandered into the room. He came over, sniffed one of Anna's shoes, then went to his birdwatching perch near the back windows. I never understood why he liked some people and not others.

Anna hadn't even noticed the cat. Her attention was still focused on the illegal activity occurring in the neighborhood. She leaned forward. "What do the police have to say about all this?"

"I haven't spoken with the police yet, but I will let them know what's been going on. Even if it doesn't have anything to do with the killings, they should be made aware of it."

"I would hope so." She frowned. "Who's behind all this?"

"That I don't know. All I've learned is that the games are arranged by email."

"*Email?*" Her frown was distasteful. "Now that's something I could never get interested in. All that computer stuff. I swear, real communication is a dying art. In another fifty years, no one will even speak to anyone else. They'll just text." She got to her feet. "Well, I'd better be on my way."

"Thank you again for the cookies, Anna."

"Oh, I was happy to do it." She started back to the front door. "It's just a shame that you couldn't find out who's organizing all this gambling. I hate knowing something like that is going on here."

"Well, if they're really interested, the police can probably discover who sent the emails. I got copies of a few of them. It wouldn't be all that difficult —"

She whirled suddenly. Her hand came out of her purse and there was a gun in it.

"I was afraid you'd say that," she said. "Get back into the kitchen."

"What are you *doing*?"

"Go on. Get in there." She gestured with the gun. It was a very small automatic, but I didn't doubt it could do a lot of damage. "Go on over to the garage door. You're going to have a tragic accident."

"But why — It was you!"

"Took you long enough to figure it out." She gestured again. "Go on."

I backed into the kitchen with Anna a couple of feet behind me. I was wondering what I could use as a weapon. That's when Curtis made a sudden move to follow. He shot in front of Anna, tripping her and hurrying to his food bowl.

The hand holding the gun flew in the air as she tried to regain her balance. She grabbed for the door frame, but missed. Then she went down, instinctively using her hands to break her fall. The gun skittered across the floor and I rushed to pick it up.

"My wrist! Oh, God, I think I broke it! And my knee —"

Curtis didn't give her more than a quick curious glance. There might be an angry woman lying on the kitchen floor, but his supply of kibble was safe. He began eating.

"Help me! It hurts!"

"Shut up, Anna." I was breathing hard.

"You've got to help me. I'm hurt!"

"I don't have to do anything at all but call the police." I eased past her, careful not to get close enough for her to grab me.

I hurried to the office where I'd left my phone and quickly dialed 911. As it rang, I went back where I could keep an eye on Anna. I quickly told the operator what happened.

"Are you in danger now?" she asked.

"No. She's out of commission, I think. And I've got the gun."

"Please stay on the line, ma'am. I have an officer en route and an ambulance."

I put the phone on speaker and set it on the counter just above Anna's head, but I kept the gun in my right hand.

"The police are on the way with an ambulance," I told Anna.

"Could you at least help me sit up?" Her voice was weak and breathy. "I'm having a hard time breathing. I won't try anything, really."

I didn't believe her helpless, weak, little old lady act for a minute, but she did seem to be hurt. Her right hand lay on the floor, bent to one side at an unnatural angle.

"If you try to hurt me, I'll kick you in the knee," I told her.

After putting the gun well out of reach on the opposite counter, I lifted her torso up from the floor. She held her wrist with her left hand and moaned. When she was leaning back against a cabinet with her legs out in front of her, I stepped quickly away from her.

"It hurts so bad!" she said. "At least get me pillow to put under my wrist."

"I think we'll just wait for the ambulance," I told her. Catering to a double murderer wasn't something I wanted to do.

"Why are you being so mean to me?" Her face crumpled and I thought she was going to cry.

"Why am *I* being mean? You're the one who was going to shoot me!"

She tried for innocence. "I wouldn't have shot you."

"No, you probably wouldn't have. You like bashing people over the head, don't you? What was that tragic accident you were planning for me? Was I going to reach for something heavy on a top shelf and have it fall and kill me?"

She looked at the floor and I knew I was right. "I just wanted some more information from you. I wasn't going to hurt you."

"Really? You've already killed two people. Why would you stop with me?"

She sighed. "They didn't give me any choice! Sarah couldn't have been happier when I set up those games. And she sure did love that I extended her credit so she could keep playing, even when she ran out of money." She gave a little gasp when she slightly shifted a leg, inadvertently moving her hand.

"Sounds like she was a great customer. Why did you kill her?"

"I didn't mean to!" she said angrily. "I went to talk to her after the game that night, to work out some kind of payment plan. She owed me over $5,000! But she wouldn't even discuss it. She said Owen would find out if she took any more money out of savings.

"The little fool actually she thought she could win it back! And … and she wanted to play with house money until she got even again. Gamblers are so *stupid*." Anna sounded outraged. "Who *does* that? Did she think I'd run a business that way?"

"Why didn't you just write it off as a bad debt?" I looked out the window, but there was no sign of a patrol car or an ambulance.

"I would have." She took a deep breath and closed her eyes for a moment. She certainly wasn't faking the pain. "I tried! Told her that she couldn't play until she paid up, but that was all. It's not like I'd send someone to collect from her. But that wasn't good enough for the little bitch. She threatened to tell the police about my games if I didn't let her to keep playing." She looked up at me beseechingly. "Could I *please* have a glass of water? I think I'm going to faint."

She did look awfully pale, but nothing would make me trust her. I sure wasn't going to give her a glass that she could smash and use as a weapon. I opened an upper cabinet and reached behind the glasses to retrieve a plastic cup. I filled it with a few ounces of water, then stretched my arm out to hand it to Anna.

She looked up at me with disgust. "What do you think I'm going to do, Emily? Drown you in a cup of water?"

"Who knows what you're capable of? You killed Sarah with a lamp."

She took a few sips of the water and put the cup on the floor beside her. "I told you I didn't mean to kill her. She just made me so furious. If she reported the games to the police, it would have ruined me! I have a reputation to maintain. I had a long, successful career and I've done quite well with the gambling, too. And that insipid woman, who'd never done anything significant in her life, thought she could take all that away from me."

"So you killed her with a lamp."

"I didn't mean to *kill* her." She paused to take a breath. "She was making these threats and I was angry and I picked up the first thing that came to hand!"

I was pretty sure that a 10 to 15-pound chunk of pink Himalayan salt wasn't the "first thing that came to hand," but I wasn't going to argue with her. I wanted to hear everything she'd tell me before the police arrived. One reason she was speaking so freely, I thought, was to keep her mind off the pain. Once the ambulance and police got there and began treating her injuries, she might decide not to say anything else.

Since I wasn't acting as an agent for the police, I wasn't required to give her any warnings about self-incrimination. And I could testify to everything she told me.

"Did Becky make you angry, too?"

She shook her head. "No, she just came waltzing in the front door like it was the middle of the day. Didn't even knock! I never knew why. Maybe she and Sarah were going to have a drink after the party. Hell, maybe it was their regular little thing! I don't know. All I know is she walked in the house and right into the room where we were."

"So you killed her, too?" I asked incredulously.

"I just wanted to talk to her. But she saw Sarah lying there and took off. I followed her back to her house. What else could I do?"

"I'm surprised you didn't shoot her," I said dryly.

Her mouth tightened. "I didn't have a gun with me. It's not like I expected trouble that night."

"So what happened?"

"I'm not as quick as I used to be." She frowned. "By the time I got there, she was slamming the front door. I heard the lock click." She gave me a crafty look. "But everybody knew she kept a spare key under the welcome mat. Not the smartest hiding place. I got it and just unlocked the door. She was digging around in her purse — for her phone, I guess — when I came in the house."

"What was the first thing that came to hand that time?" I asked.

She narrowed her eyes, obviously not appreciating my sarcasm. "She rushed at me. It was self defense. I had to hit her with that tacky figurine to protect myself."

"Ummmm. I'm sure." I didn't bother to correct her. I knew and the police knew that Becky was killed in the back of the house, not the entrance hall. She wasn't rushing Anna, she was trying to get away from her.

"There's just one thing that confuses me. Why did you lock Sarah's door and then take the keys?"

"After I . . . left Becky, I went back to Sarah's house. I had to look through her things in the office. For all I knew, she kept records of our transactions."

"Did you find anything?"

"No." She held out the cup. "I need some more water."

I wasn't going to be distracted. "But why lock the door?"

She shrugged, then winced when the movement caused her pain. "It just seemed like a good idea at the time. You know, just to confuse the situation."

I was listening for an approaching vehicle. Even if they didn't run the sirens in the neighborhood, I thought I might hear the engines. Ambulances are noisy things. It had been almost seven minutes since they were dispatched. Surely they'd get there soon. I wasn't sure how much more of Anna I could take. And there wasn't anything else I wanted to ask.

I was filling the cup a second time when I heard a loud engine and footsteps on the walk. I picked up the phone.

"They're here," I told the 911 operator. "Did you get all that?"

"Every word, ma'am."

"Thanks."

I took the gun into the foyer with me, but set it on the console table before I opened the door.

TWENTY-FOUR

THE EMTS, TWO YOUNG MEN, ONE BLACK AND ONE WHITE, were first in the door. They were closely followed by two patrol officers, a thirtyish woman with short blond hair and a slightly older, thickly-built man. His name tag identified him as W. O. Massey. The woman's name was Langford.

The officers stood beside me in the foyer while the techs went straight to Anna.

"Broken wrist," one said.

Within minutes they had her wrist immobilized and were checking out the rest of her. Anna kept up a constant stream of demands, complaints, and accusations against me.

"She attacked me for no reason! I want to press charges! Oh, it hurts! It really hurts! Can't you be more careful?"

The officers looked at me.

"She was pointing that gun at me when she fell." I gestured toward the console table where the pistol lay.

"You're the one who called 911, ma'am?"

"Yes." I gave them my name. "That's Anna Lumpkin. She came here to find out what I knew about the two murders in the neighborhood. When she realized I was going to tell the police what I'd learned, she pulled that gun out of her purse. I have no doubt she was going to shoot me. She's already killed two other people."

"That little old lady?" Langford asked, unbelieving.

"You don't know the half of what she's done."

"Her knee looks like it's sprained and she may have cracked a rib or two," one EMT told Massey. "Won't know 'til we get her in."

A few minutes later, they loaded her onto a gurney more carefully than I would have and wheeled her out the door.

"I thought she'd never leave," I said. I could feel hysteria bubbling up and took a deep breath to try and calm myself.

Massey ignored my comment. Instead he said, "The detectives assigned to the murder cases are on their way."

"Webster and Engels?" I asked.

"Yeah. Should be here in a little while."

I nodded. "Can we at least sit down while we wait?"

"Sure." He nodded to the chairs at the dining room table. "Just don't touch anything."

I didn't want to touch anything. I just wanted to sit, put my head on my arms and not move. I couldn't remember ever feeling so exhausted. That's what happens when the adrenaline wears off.

All I could see of Curtis was the tip of his tail, sticking out from behind the plant in the corner. There were entirely too many unfamiliar people and too much activity in the house for his liking.

When Engels and Webster showed up, they didn't ring the bell. They just walked in and I realized my house was now considered a crime scene. Langford went to meet them. I couldn't hear what was being said, but I saw her gesture toward the console table. Webster moved closer to get a better look at the gun.

When he and Engels came into the dining room, I started to get to my feet, but Buddy waved a hand.

"Sit down, Emily." He pulled out a chair next to me. Engels stood a few feet away, leaning against the door frame. "Just relax. We heard what happened."

"Yeah, I saw the officer telling you —"

"No, we *heard* what happened. It was all recorded by the 911 system. They played it back for us while we were driving here. The quality isn't great, but it was good enough to hear that woman confess to two murders." He grinned. "You did good, the way you kept her talking."

Engels nodded, but didn't make any comment.

"As far as I can see, all we need to do is take the gun and you can get back to your life."

"Don't you need to process the scene?"

"She broke her wrist during the commission of a felony, didn't she? What else do we need to know?"

Engels had already pulled on gloves. She picked up the gun, dropped it into a plastic evidence bag, and sealed it. Then she wrote what I knew were her initials across the seal. They'd log it into evidence as soon as they got back to the office.

"Just one thing," he said. "How did you take her down if she had the gun on you?"

"It wasn't me," I told him. "It was Curtis."

He looked around for another person.

"Curtis. He's a cat." I took him over to the plant and pointed down. Curtis glared up at him. "She was holding the gun on me, told me to go into the kitchen. I think she was planning to kill me in the garage. But Curtis tripped her. I just grabbed the gun when she dropped it."

Engels burst out laughing. "So *you* didn't do anything. Your cat captured a double murderer while you just stood there."

"Yep. That's what happened."

I didn't try to make it sound any better than it was. Engels was really enjoying the situation and I knew that the story of my cat's heroics (and my lack of action) would be all over the department by sunset. But I was so glad to be alive and have the case closed that I didn't care.

"Do you want to take my statement now?"

Buddy laughed. "I think we can trust you to write your own statement, Emily. Just drop it by sometime this weekend. I'd say you could email it, but we need the original signature."

I promised they'd have the statement the next day. Webster and Engels left the house, taking the gun with them. The patrol officers were right behind them.

I followed them out and saw that the neighborhood carnival had moved to our cul-de-sac. The ambulance and police cars had drawn my neighbors like moths to a flame. Nick and Linda stood at the end of the driveway. When they saw me, they hurried to where I was.

"Are you okay?" Nick asked, looking me over to be sure I wasn't injured.

"They wouldn't let us in," Linda said indignantly. "Even when we told them we were your friends, they said we couldn't come in!"

"Who was in the ambulance?"

"What happened?"

I held up a hand. "Come in and I'll tell you all about it."

TWENTY-FIVE

TEN MINUTES LATER, WE'D ALL GOTTEN COMFORTABLE IN the living room with tall glasses of iced tea at hand. Linda and Nick were impatient to hear what had happened, but I was perfectly happy taking my time to wrap it up for them. Having all the drama behind me gave me an unexpected feeling of leisure.

"Who was in the ambulance?" Linda asked.

"Anna Lumpkin."

"The woman from Owen's neighborhood? What happened to her?"

"Well, she brought me some cookies to thank me for looking into the murders, and then pulled a gun on me."

"A gun?" Nick asked. "Are you sure you're okay?"

"I'm fine."

"But why did she do that? Was she having some kind of mental breakdown?"

"It sure sounds like it," Linda said. "Cookies and a gun are a pretty strange combination."

I drank some tea, enjoying the knowledge that it was all over. "The cookies were just an excuse for her to come and try to find out what I knew about the Marchpoint gambling."

"What difference did it make to her?" Linda asked.

"At first I thought she was just nosy, wanting to find out what was going on so she could tell all her friends." I looked at Linda with a grin. "You know how important it is to be the first one with the latest news."

Linda smiled ruefully.

"But that wasn't it?" Nick asked.

"Nope. It seems she was the one running the neighborhood gambling parties."

"No!" Linda said.

"Yep. Evidently retirement bored her. Somehow, she learned that Sarah and the others were going up to North Carolina to gamble. The women I talked to all said they kept it a secret, but you know how secrets are, especially in this neighborhood.

"And that gave her an idea of how to make some money. She'd spent a lot of years in the business world. This was just a case of supply and demand. She teamed up with some casino workers in Cherokee — I'm sure their employers had no idea what they were doing — to set up the games here in Marchpoint. And she was really smart about it. Made all the arrangements anonymously through email."

Nick was shaking his head in disbelief. "All that was happening here, right in front of the whole neighborhood, and nobody noticed it?"

"Well, people were talking ..."

"Oh, yes," Linda said, "everybody knew about the parties, but no one was sure exactly what was going on."

"Yeah," I said, smiling, "there were some wild stories going around. And as long as that's all it was, just speculation and gossip, Anna wasn't worried. But the murders changed the stakes for her."

"So when we found the game Wednesday night, it must have scared her. She was afraid she was going to get caught?" Linda asked.

"Yeah, that and having me going around asking questions. Not that I found out anything about the murders. I told her today that we didn't know who ran the organization and that was that. She was ready to leave. But I made the mistake of mentioning I planned to tell the police about the games."

Curtis poked his head around the plant. Reassured when he saw only friendly faces, he crossed to the sofa, jumped up and sat between Nick and me. He stretched, lay down and closed his eyes. Just another day in his neighborhood.

"Even that wasn't a problem for her," I said. "But then I told her I had copies of the emails and thought the police would probably be able track whoever sent them. That's when she pulled a gun on me."

Linda gasped. "Oh, my God, I still can't believe she did that. You could have been killed!"

"But I wasn't. I'm okay."

"And that's when she got hurt?" Linda asked. "What did you do to her?"

I laughed. "It wasn't me. It was Curtis."

"He attacked her?" Nick asked incredulously.

"Not exactly." I gave the cat's head a good rubbing. "He walked right in front of her to get to his food bowl. She tripped over him and went down really hard."

"Good cat," Nick said, stroking his back.

With two people petting him simultaneously, life was very good for Curtis. His purr was resounding.

"He deserves a reward!" Linda said.

"Yeah, I think he's assured himself of an ongoing supply of tuna," Nick declared.

I continued with my story. "When she fell, she broke her wrist and maybe some other things. And she dropped the gun. I picked it up and called 911. From then on, we just waited for the ambulance. She told me she killed Sarah and Becky, but insisted she didn't mean to. She called them accidents."

"Accidents?" Linda exclaimed. "She hit Sarah over the head with a gigantic block of salt!"

"Yeah. I don't think that story's going to hold up."

"But why go after the other woman?" Nick asked.

"Becky walked into the house right after Anna killed Sarah and saw what had happened, so Anna followed her home and took her out, too."

They both had more questions, but I had to put them off for a few minutes. There were a couple of calls that needed to be made. I retrieved my phone from the kitchen and dialed Owen's number.

"It's over," I told him and gave him a condensed version of what had happened.

"That's fantastic! Can I take this thing off my ankle now?"

"You know you can't. It has to be done by the people who put it on."

"But nobody's called me."

"They will, Owen, this just happened. Believe me, you'll be off house arrest by tomorrow, maybe sooner. Call Bishop and give him a heads up. And after you tell Drew, make sure you call Chelsea. And I mean right now! She's been horribly upset."

"I will, I will. Emily, how can I thank you?"

"Just let the kids know everything's okay."

My mother took the news calmly. "Well, I always knew Owen couldn't have done what you said. I'm just glad it's over. After all that's happened, do you think the two of you might get back together?"

"No."

I rejoined the others in the living room and we talked a bit longer. Then Linda took her glass to the kitchen. "There's so much more I want to ask you, but I have to go. Angel needs to be walked. I'll see y'all later."

"After the walk," I said, "why don't you bring her back here with you? We'll get something to eat and make a night of it."

Nick was frowning. "What about the cat?"

"Oh, she and Curtis are pals," Linda said. She gave me a big smile. "That's a super idea!"

She was back in half an hour with Angel.

"She's doing great on the leash," I said, watching Linda unhook it from her collar.

"Yeah, it took some getting used to, but she doesn't mind it at all now."

As soon as she was free, Angel ran into the living room in search of the cat. Curtis was still sleeping on the sofa, but woke when he heard her. Minutes later, the two were rolling around together on the floor. Neither seemed to know they were supposed to be natural enemies.

"That's great!" Nick said, watching them with a big smile on his face. "They act like they've been friends all their lives."

"Well, they bonded during the tornado," Linda told him.

We ordered in pizza—loaded for us, vegetarian for Linda—and she insisted on paying for it.

"It's the least I can do after you put that cool camera in my doorbell," she told Nick.

Excitedly, she showed me the app on her phone as Nick provided technical information.

"You can program it for various distances," he said. "Most people have it set up so that if someone comes near the door, say within 10 feet, you get an alarm on your phone."

"Yes, and you can see them—right there! It's like a little movie," Linda said. "And you can tell them to get away from your house."

"Yeah, there's a microphone and speaker built into the device," Nick said.

This gadget was sounding more impressive all the time. I was looking forward to having Nick install the one he'd ordered for me.

"But he set mine for a larger area!"

"Right," Nick said. "I think it's about 30 feet."

"So I get an alarm whenever anyone approaches my mailbox!" Linda said. "I'll be able to see the stalker when he puts things in it!"

I voiced the same objection I'd shared earlier with Nick. "But won't it drive you crazy if you get an alarm when anyone gets near your mailbox? There must be a hundred people a day walking past your house."

Walking was the exercise of choice in Marchpoint, and at all hours. I had friends who chose to get their workout around midnight.

"I know!" she said, brightly. "I've already gotten a bunch of alarms today. But all I have to do is look at the phone. If it's a walker, I just delete them."

I wasn't sure I'd want to be notified that often, but Linda was absolutely chipper about it. I was just glad she was feeling more secure.

"It's so great! You just wait and see. I'm going to catch this pervert!"

The device worked well. So well, in fact, that she was interrupted several times during dinner. She shared the videos with us—our neighbors walking past her house, none of them with any idea they were being watched.

Drew came for lunch Saturday.

"I like what you've done with the house," he told me.

I laughed. "Yeah, it looks a little different than the last time you were here."

He'd spent a weekend months ago helping me move in. It was the last time he'd been in Georgia until this week.

Over sandwiches, I learned that Mike Bishop had been very busy. He arranged for the police to drop the charges against Owen and had gotten the ankle bracelet off the evening before.

"I don't think I've ever seen Dad so happy." He smiled at me. "And it's all because of you, Mom. We'll never be able to thank you enough."

"I'm just glad it's over."

"Me, too. We're going out for a celebration dinner tonight. Dad's so excited to get out! He's made reservations at The Caribou."

"Sounds wonderful. How long are you going to be staying?"

He shook his head. "I've got to get back. Dad's taking me to the airport in the morning. Then he's driving up to see Chelsea and the kids tomorrow afternoon. She's been so worried! He just wants to make her feel better."

"I wish you could stay longer, but I understand."

"Yeah, it would have been nice to meet Nick. But I'll be back in a couple of months for the memorial service. I'm sure we can get together then."

"Service? For Sarah?"

"That's right. They're releasing the body this week and we made arrangements for the cremation at Funderburke's Funeral Home."

Knowing Owen, I'd be willing to bet that there was no *we* involved. Either Drew or Sarah's daughter in Jacksonville had done the planning.

"The service will be held there for her in June, on her birthday."

"We'll be sure and get together when you come back."

I hugged him tight before he left. It was hard having both my children live out of state, but at least Chelsea was only an hour away and we saw each other regularly. Being with Drew only once or twice a year was tough.

"I'll miss you, Drew. I love you."

"Love you, too, Mom."

Then he was gone.

On Sunday, we took another motorcycle trip — this just a short one over to Lake Oconee where we had a late lunch.

"I've been thinking," Nick said before we started for home. "Now that you're a veteran, we should take a longer ride. Maybe the Blue Ridge Parkway or the Natchez Trace."

I surprised myself by agreeing. Instead of terrifying me, it sounded like a great adventure. Amazing what a difference a week can make.

"Have you ridden either one?"

"No, although I've driven a short distance on the Parkway in a car. But I really like the idea of seeing new places with you."

TWENTY-SIX

THE NEXT FEW DAYS WERE BLESSEDLY ROUTINE IN MARCH- point. Owen's freedom was restored and news of Anna Lumpkin's villainy spread fast. Predictably, a lot of people now claimed there had always been something peculiar about Anna and everyone I spoke with declared they'd never believed Owen was guilty.

It wasn't until Wednesday that Linda sprang her trap. She showed up at my door early that afternoon, phone held high in triumph. In her other hand was an envelope.

"I got him! The proof is right here!"

Her fingers moved quickly over the screen. "There." She held the phone so I could see. "Just look."

Although the picture was small, I could easily make out her mailbox and a man opening it. As we watched, he put something inside, closed the box and quickly walked away.

"I can't believe it! That's Leo Montgomery!" I said.

"No, that's my stalker! Look what he left this time."

I took the envelope from her and pulled out the usual floral greeting card.

Thinking of you on this beautiful day.

"And now I'm calling the police!"

"Ummmm … you may want to think about that. As far as I can see, he hasn't broken the law."

"But he's stalking me!"

"No. What he's done is leave you some greeting cards. There aren't any threats or even any suggestive language in them."

"But he's putting them in the mailbox himself, not even mailing them."

I nodded. "He might be violating some obscure postal regulation, but he hasn't committed any crime that I know of."

She frowned in frustration. "Then what am I supposed to do? Just let him keep stalking me?"

I wished she wouldn't use that word so liberally. I thought for a moment.

"Why don't you confront him?"

"What? Wait until he comes back to my mailbox and yell at him?"

"That's not quite what I had in mind," I said. "You could call him or even go to his house."

"Oh, right. I'm going to go to the stalker's house so he can attack me in private. How can you even suggest something so dangerous?"

"I was thinking you might just talk to him. That's the reasonable thing to do. And I'll go with you. That way you won't be alone with him." This situation had to be resolved. "You've been too upset for too long over this. If you don't confront him, this will just go on and keep making you miserable."

She was nodding. "I know, but what if he really is crazy.?"

"I've never heard anything bad about him. And I'll be right there with you." Finally she agreed. I looked up his address in the directory. Leo Montgomery only lived a block away. We could have easily walked, but I thought having the car might be a good idea—in case things did get unpleasant and we needed to leave quickly.

Linda followed me out to the car and got in without a word. A couple of minutes later, we pulled into Leo's driveway. His house, painted a muted green, looked like all the others in the neighborhood. I opened my door, but Linda didn't move.

"I'm not sure this is such a good idea."

"Come on," I said. "Let's get it over with."

She gave an exasperated sigh. "Oh, okay."

I rang the bell and Leo answered it quickly. He was a slender man, about my height, with a halo of short gray hair surrounding a small bald spot on the top of his head. He was neatly dressed in a red polo shirt tucked into dark trousers. When he saw Linda, his face lit up like a sunrise, but that joyous expression disappeared as soon as she spoke.

"You've been sneaking around leaving cards in my mailbox! You even took a picture of me and my dog!" Her tone was withering and she was looking at him like he was something nasty that she'd stepped in.

"No … I … You don't understand." He could hardly meet her eyes. "I just wanted you to know how lovely I think you are. And the picture … I took it with my phone. It was just for me, but when I saw how pretty you looked in it, I thought you should have it."

She looked so angry that I was afraid she might actually hit him.

"Why didn't you just tell her?" I asked.

"Oh, she wouldn't want to hear anything from someone like me." He looked at Linda, then back to me. "She's like some magical creature, so beautiful and so kind. One time I saw her stop her car on Marchpoint Boulevard to rescue a turtle that was crossing the street. She picked him up so carefully and then took him down a walking trail." His eyes, brown and adoring, slid back to Linda. "You were taking him to the stream, weren't you?"

Linda nodded, her anger fading. "That's where he was going. I just helped so he didn't get run over."

"You see?" he asked me. "Someone needed to tell her how special she is, how wonderful. But I'd... she wouldn't want to hear something like that from me."

"Why not?" Linda asked.

Leo turned back to her, looking like he was almost daring to hope.

"Could we maybe come in for a minute?" I asked. I didn't think the front porch was the place for this conversation.

"Of course, of course. Forgive my rudeness. Please come in." He stepped back into the house and motioned for us to enter. Linda gave me an uncertain look, but followed me inside.

"Please, come in. Sit down. Could I get you something to drink?"

"No, thanks," I answered for both of us. "We're fine."

His living room was neat and pleasantly furnished in muted shades of green and brown. The only decorations on the walls were family photos. A recliner, obviously *his* chair, was set in a corner beside an end table stacked with books. The sofa where Linda and I sat looked untouched, the cushions perfectly rounded with no wrinkles or indentions. In fact, everything in the room looked untouched with the exception of Leo's chair.

Linda's anger had disappeared. "I still don't understand why you left the cards for me," she said.

He pursed his lips for a moment, trying to find the right words, then said, "When I went in for my physical last year, my doctor told me I needed to get more exercise. My wife and I used to go hiking all the time." His eyes strayed to a picture of an attractive woman on the far wall. "But then she passed away. It's been six years now and I guess I just hadn't found anything else I liked to do."

Linda's face was a study in sympathy.

"But the doctor was pretty adamant about it, so I started walking. It's easy and you can do it any time. And this is a good place to walk. There's almost no traffic and people always say hello." He smiled. "I take the same route, so a lot of the time, I see the same people. It's nice. Friendly, I guess, is the word for it."

"I've seen you," Linda said. "You walk right by my house."

"Yes! And if you're outside, you always say hello."

"Then why didn't you stop and talk to me?"

"You're just so … amazing." He laughed self-consciously. "So far out of my league. I knew you wouldn't want to talk to someone like me."

"You keep saying that, Leo. You must think I'm really shallow."

"Oh, no! But, you're so special. I couldn't just start talking to you. But then at Christmas my daughter gave me a box of greeting cards." He smiled. "The kids never know what to get me. Usually they just settle for gift certificates to restaurants. But this year, for some reason, she gave me the box of cards. Of course, I don't write to anyone, so they just sat on my desk.

"Then one day, when I passed your house and saw you getting your mail, I had this idea. I could send you a card and you'd know that someone thought you were special."

"And that way you wouldn't have to work up the nerve to actually speak to her," I said.

Color rose in his face. "Yeah, that, too. So I started leaving those cards in her mailbox." He looked at Linda. "In *your* mailbox."

She shook her head. "Oh, Leo, why didn't you just say something? Look at all the time you wasted with those silly cards, time we could have been friends."

He stared at her for a long minute, astonishment on his face. "We could have been friends?"

She pushed out a frustrated breath. "We still can be, Leo!"

She jumped up and started toward him. He stood at the same time. They met in the middle of the room and Linda stuck out her hand.

"Hello, I'm Linda Winkler."

He shook her hand. "Uh...Hi, I'm Leo Montgomery."

"See," Linda said. "That wasn't so hard, was it? Now when you're walking and I'm outside, you can stop and we'll talk because we're friends."

He was grinning now. "I'd like that. Do you think I could meet your dog, too?"

"Angel. Her name is Angel and of course, you can meet her. Maybe sometimes we can all walk together."

The drive back to my place was considerably more pleasant than the earlier one had been.

"He actually seemed nice," Linda said. "Poor man. You can tell he's been so lonely since his wife died. And I can sympathize with that."

I smiled at her. "He didn't seem threatening at all, did he?"

"Of course not," she said. She was now Leo's defender. "He's just terribly shy."

"Maybe you can help him with that."

"Well, it is the neighborly thing to do."

Linda seemed happier and more upbeat than she had in weeks. But it didn't last. Monday afternoon she came to my house with tears rolling down her face with the dog on a leash. She came in, dropped the leash and threw herself in my arms, sobbing as if her heart was broken.

As I held her, a parade of horrible possibilities ran through my mind. Was someone dead? Was she sick? I'd never seen her like this.

She finally pulled back and, with shaking hands, took the leash off the dog's collar. But this time Angel didn't run to find Curtis. She stayed right beside Linda.

"What is it? Are you hurt?"

She took a shaky breath. "It's Angel!"

"What? Is she sick?"

"No. Not her. Me!"

"*You're* sick?"

She nodded. "I'm allergic!" With that she was hit with another spasm of tears, but she managed to choke out four words. "I'm ... allergic ... to *her!*"

She couldn't seem to stop crying, but she let me lead her to the sofa. After I'd brought out a box of tissues and she'd blown her nose a couple of times, she was finally able to speak again. "I went to the doctor and he referred me to an allergist. The appointment was this morning and he did these tests. You know, the kind where they scratch your skin with a bunch of needles?"

I nodded to show I did.

"Then he told me." She swallowed hard to hold the tears back.

"I'm allergic to dogs! I can't live with her anymore. Allergic to my Angel!"

Here came the tears again. While she cried, Angel sat at her feet, those big, brown eyes never leaving Linda's face. I put an arm around her shoulders.

"But that's not the end of the world. There must be things you can do. Medicine, even shots. It doesn't mean you have to give up your dog."

She gulped again, reached for a tissue and blew her nose. "I know, I know, but he said that my allergy is really severe and, with my asthma, it could be dangerous."

I remembered that she'd had asthma when she was younger, but it had been under control for years.

She put a loving hand on the little dog's head. "They can do the shots, but it'll take a couple of weeks for them to get the serum and, even then, it could be weeks or even a month before it takes effect and builds up my immunity. He said...if she's in the house with me, especially if she's in my bedroom during that time, it could trigger a bad attack. He said he wouldn't be responsible for what happened!"

She teared up again. "Emily, I can't give her away, I just can't. I love her so."

"Can she go back to your house after your immunity has been built up?"

"I guess. But there are all these rules. I have to keep taking the shots and she has to get regular baths and I can't give them to her. She'd have to go to a groomer. And she can't be in the bedroom ever again. Poor baby, she just loves snuggling with me at night." She reached down to pet the dog again. "Don't you, Angel? You love sleeping with Mommy."

"Okay, that gives us something to work with," I said. "We'll figure this out, Linda. It's going to be okay."

I made us each a cup of tea and we sat at the kitchen table to drink it and work our way through the problem. Linda was calmer now. Angel had found Curtis, stretched out in front of the fridge where he could take advantage of the heat coming from the motor. The puppy joined him there and was welcomed by a few ear licks. Then he went back to sleep and she curled up beside him and did the same.

"Now let me make sure I understand. Angel has to move out of your house for a while until the allergy shots have done their work."

She nodded, still looking miserable.

"And," I went on, "when she comes back, she has to have regular grooming and can't come in the bedroom. Is that about it?"

"Yeah, you make it sound so simple, but it isn't." Tears were threatening again. "Even if I could afford it, I can't board her somewhere that long. She'd be miserable and she might even forget me!"

"Why can't she stay with me?" I nodded to the two animals sleeping peacefully beside each other. "Curtis would love it."

"I couldn't ask you to do that, Emily. Taking care of a dog is a lot of work, especially Angel. She's used to getting bunches of attention and she has to be walked four or five times a day."

"Well, as for attention, I'll be happy to give her all she wants, but I think Curtis will take over most of that job. And why can't you walk her? Of course I'll take her out first thing in the morning and before I go to bed at night, but you could do the rest, couldn't you? Just walking with her shouldn't set off an asthma attack. And even if she's not living with you can still see her. I know you don't want to lose your relationship with her."

Linda was smiling for the first time since she walked in the door. "I could do that, of course, I could. I'd love to! And it would only be until the shots have had time to work."

I was nodding. "And in the meantime, you can find a groomer to give her a weekly bath. There are some that'll come right to your house. I've seen their vans in the neighborhood.

"And you'll have plenty of time to deep clean your bedroom — carpet, comforter, curtains, everything. Get rid of all that dog hair and dander. That should help, too."

Linda looked over at Angel and her face grew sad again. "But she'll expect to sleep with me when she comes home. She won't understand."

"Animals are like people, Linda. They're adaptable. Don't you think she'd rather do that than lose you?"

"Well, when you put it that way …"

"There's no other way to put it. This is going to work out just fine. Go home and call the allergist. Tell them you want to take the shots so they can get started making the serum. Then you can bring Angel over this evening. And her food and her bed, if she has one."

"Okay, I'll call him." She swallowed hard again. "But I can't bring Angel over until tomorrow morning. We need one last night together."

"Don't you dare start crying again. This is not goodbye, it's just see you later."

TWENTY-SEVEN

THE LAST SUNDAY IN MAY DAWNED CLEAR AND DRY, BUT clouds were building in the west when Nick and I arrived at Scott and Annette's house just after four. A light breeze was blowing from that direction and I crossed my fingers that the blue skies overhead would stay with us until the wedding was over.

I was wearing the dress Ariel had chosen for me and it had already provoked several admiring looks from Nick. With stacked-heel sandals and a small beige clutch, I thought it was an acceptable outfit for the big day.

Nick had chosen a blue suit for the occasion and, a rarity for him, a yellow tie.

When I'd expressed my surprise at the tie, he'd just shrugged. "You have to dress right for a wedding."

We walked down the drive to the backyard where the guests had gathered.

"Who's performing the ceremony?" he asked.

"Emory Ferris."

"The District Attorney? I didn't know performing marriages was one of the duties that came with the office."

"It isn't. But he really likes Annette. When she asked him, he went online and got the credentials to do it."

The backyard had been transformed. An archway, covered with foliage and flowers, had been erected in the shade of two big oak trees. Rows of chairs were set up on the left and right sides of the arch, creating a short aisle between them.

Across the yard were three long tables loaded with covered dishes. Two women in kitchen whites stood behind them. I now understood why Annette hadn't needed me to make potato salad. Ariel had gotten her way with both the caterers and the decorations.

Nick spotted a couple of people he knew and joined them while I went to the house to find Annette. It was a small wedding and, as the bride's only attendant, I just had one duty. I was responsible for the ring she'd be slipping on Scott's finger. My own fingers touched the soft cloth of my clutch, feeling the reassuring presence of the ring. There was a second object in the purse as well. I'd brought the fairy cross with me. Scott and Annette deserved all the good fortune in the world and I was happy to share.

I walked in the back door to find Ariel in the kitchen, looking down at the yard below. When she saw me, her face lit with a smile.

"Emily, you look lovely! Oh, I knew that was the right color for you."

We hugged. "Thank you, Ariel. It's beautiful. I love it! But I still wish you'd let me pay you for it."

We'd had this discussion several times over the past month and she was a remarkably stubborn woman.

"Absolutely not. It's my pleasure." She glanced back out the window. "Did you see the yard?"

"I did. Very nice."

"I think the arch just makes it, don't you? Annette didn't want to do it, but I kept insisting. After all, this is the only wedding she's ever going to have. I believe even she's happy with it now." She gave me a wink. "Come on. Let's go find her."

Annette was in her bedroom. She turned when we entered and, for a moment, I could do nothing but stare at her.

"You look incredible!"

She grinned self-consciously. "Yeah, Mama did good with the dress."

It wasn't typical attire for a bride. The dress was a pale, shimmering lavender. Elegantly draped over her body, cut low in the front and back, it hugged every curve. Her braids were piled high on her head, spilling down here and there. She looked like a Greek statue come to life.

Ariel walked across the room and put an arm around her shoulders. "Isn't my baby beautiful?"

"She surely is."

Annette's two white standard poodles sat near the bed, well behaved as always. Each dog wore a black satin bow tie around his neck.

"Love the ties," I said.

Annette laughed. "Jules and Jacques don't like them very much, but they haven't tried to get them off yet."

At 4:30 exactly, we left the bedroom. Ariel handed each of us a single white rose tied with a pale green ribbon. Then she went out the door and down the steps to the yard where she would to be seated in a place of honor as the mother of the bride.

Annette called the dogs. They came obediently and she opened the back door.

"Let's go outside," she told them.

That was all the encouragement they needed. They bounded down the steps to investigate the activity in below. I thought I heard a distant rumble of thunder, but the sun was still shining brightly. So far, so good.

"Ready?" I asked Annette.

"I think so." She gave a nervous giggle. "Can you believe I'm doing this?"

"It's about time. You and Scott are perfect for each other."

We carefully made our way down to the yard to where the guests waited. There seemed to be about forty people seated in the chairs near the arch. As we neared them, everyone stood. I led the way as an attendant was supposed to do, down the aisle between the chairs to the archway where Emory Ferris waited.

He was a heavy-set man in his fifties with bright eyes and a cheerful expression; he looked like everyone's favorite uncle. But I'd seen him in action. That cheerful expression could turn deadly serious in a heartbeat. You didn't want to be his adversary in a courtroom.

Scott stood to Emory's left with his best man, his brother, Ken. I took my place opposite them, then turned to watch Annette walk slowly down the short aisle.

When Scott saw her, a look of amazement spread across his face. For a moment, he looked like he'd forgotten how to breathe. Then he gave her a smile that was full of love.

Annette handed me her rose, then the couple took their place in front of Emory. He began by welcoming the families and guests. There was another roll of thunder, a little closer this time, but no one paid attention to it. All eyes were focused on the people beneath the flowered arch.

The ceremony was short and simple, just the way Annette and Scott planned it. The ring hand-off went without a hitch and the vows were lovingly exchanged. But, before Emory could finish, rain started to fall.

To call it rain is a significant understatement. The darkness was sudden and the skies opened. Huge drops fell and the guests started leaving their seats, looking for shelter. The caterers were trying to cover the tables with their bodies. But Scott held up his hands.

"Please! Please! Let us finish!" He had to raise his voice to be heard over the downpour. "It's taken me a long time to convince this wonderful woman to marry me. I'm not going to let a little rain stop it."

Annette grinned, several of her braids came loose under the weight of the rain and rivulets of water ran down her face. "Yes! Let's do it!"

Emory looked at both of them like they'd gone insane, but took a deep breath and said, "By the power vested in me, I now pronounce you husband and wife."

Standing in the deluge with soaking wet friends and family looking on, Scott took Annette in his arms for a truly remarkable kiss. That seemed to be the signal Jules and Jacques were waiting for. The two big dogs ran at full speed from the other side of the yard, straight for the happy couple. They leaped and a second later, the bride and groom and the dogs collapsed into a wet tangle on the ground. The rain continued to pour. Kisses were exchanged all around and joyous laughter rang out.

I do love a happy ending.

About the Author

JACLYN WELDON WHITE IS THE AUTHOR OF TEN BOOKS, IN-cluding novels, true crimes, biographies, gardening, and travel. *The Witch of Ben Hill County* was the first in a mystery series set in an over-55, active-adult community in northeast Georgia. The second novel in that series is *The Fairy Crosses of Fannin County*.

Jaclyn was a police officer for six years, working both in street patrol and the detective division, before becoming the administrator of a large metropolitan Atlanta juvenile court. She held that position for sixteen years.

Jaclyn also designs and crafts kiln-fired silver jewelry. She has three living children and seven grandchildren, and lives in Hoschton, Georgia with three cats, two of which were planned. She is working on her third book in the County series.